ELEVEN KIDS, ONE SUMMER

ONE SUMMER

Ann M. Martin

AN
APPLE
PAPERBACK

SCHOLASTIC INC.
New York Toronto London Auckland Sydney

For Jacques d'Amboise
and all his kids,
with respect and admiration.

ISBN 0-590-45917-1

24 23 22 21 20 19 18 17 16 15 14   0 1 2/0

Printed in the U.S.A.   40

First Scholastic printing, June 1993

Contents

ELEVEN KIDS, ONE SUMMER

1

Abigail and the Train-Trip Disaster

The train started with a jerk and pulled out of the station. Abbie Rosso breathed a sigh of relief. As she looked out the window, she could see her father standing in the parking lot by the van, which was packed to the gills. Mr. Rosso was waving and smiling.

Abbie decided to take a head count. Thank goodness. The Rossos were right where they ought to be. Every one of them. Her brother Bainbridge was sitting next to her. Candy and Hannah were across the aisle. Woody and Hardy were in the seat in front of her. Faustine and Dinnie, the twins, were across from them. And farther ahead were Ira and Jan, their mother, Keegan, and Zsa-Zsa the cat, meowing in her carrier.

"All present and accounted for," murmured Abbie.

"Huh?" replied Bainbridge. He had bought a copy of *The Nation's Enquirer* at the newsstand at the train station and was deeply engrossed. Ordinarily, Mrs. Rosso didn't allow her children to buy tabloids, but she'd made an exception for the long trip ahead. Abbie peered over Bainbridge's arm. He was reading an article titled "Two-headed Calf Saves Injured Chicken."

"Hey, Mom!" yelled Woody from his seat. "You got the gum?"

"No, I have it," replied Abbie. "And keep your voice down."

She rummaged around in her tote bag for the gum they'd brought along and tossed a pack to her brother.

Bainbridge let out a loud snort. "It says here that this guy saw the face of Elvis Presley glowing on the front of his refrigerator, so he went to get his wife, but when they came back the face was gone!"

"Bainbridge, shhh!" said Abbie.

Honestly, the worst thing about having ten brothers and sisters was that it could be so em*bar*rassing. Especially when you'd been named in alphabetical order using a "name your baby" book according to a system developed by your mother. That was how Abbie and her brothers and sisters had ended up with names like Bainbridge and Faustine—and worse. Mrs. Rosso had a rule or a system for just about everything, and the baby-naming system worked like this: Abbie, the oldest child, had been given the first name on the A page in the girls' half of the book. Bainbridge had been given the second name on the B page in the boys' half. Candy had been given the third name on the C page in the girls' half, and so on down to Keegan, the baby, who'd been given the eleventh name on the boys' K page.

Most of the kids had nicknames, thank goodness, because some of their real names were pretty awful. Abbie was short for Abigail, which was a nice name. Candy was short for Calandra, which was a romantic name. Woody, however, was short for Dagwood, Hardy for Eberhard, Dinnie for Gardenia, and Jan for Janthina, which everyone agreed were terrible names. And there was nothing Bainbridge, Faustine, Hannah, Ira, or Keegan could be shortened to. In some cases it didn't matter. Hannah and Ira liked their names, and Keegan was too little to care about his.

There was another thing about the Rossos and their mother's systems. The kids had all been born a year apart, so, at least until the twins came along, they were like stairsteps. That was what Mrs. Rosso had always wanted—ten stairstep children. (Abbie thought of the twins as a landing on the stairs so as not to spoil the image.) This worked fine with the first ten children. Abbie was now fifteen, Bainbridge fourteen, Candy thirteen, Woody twelve, Hardy eleven, Faustine and Dinnie ten, Hannah nine, Ira eight, and Jan seven. Then Keegan had come along. He didn't fit into the stairsteps at all. He was only six months old. What did that make him? Hannah, who liked to tease and play jokes, said it made Keegan a pile of laundry at the bottom of the stairs, but Abbie didn't think that was funny at all.

"Meow, meow," cried Zsa-Zsa pitifully.

"Mommy? Are we almost there?" called Jan. She wiggled out of her seat and squeezed herself between Zsa-Zsa's carrier and her mother, who was holding a sleeping Keegan in her lap.

"Not yet, honey," replied Mrs. Rosso. "Remember? I said it would be a long trip. We have quite a few hours to go."

The Rossos were on their way to Fire Island, which is a narrow spit of land off the coast of Long Island in New York. They'd boarded the train in New Jersey and were traveling to Pennsylvania Station in New York City.

When they reached the station, Abbie, her mom, and her ten brothers and sisters would have to get off the train—with Zsa-Zsa, their tote bags and pocketbooks and knapsacks, and Keegan's diaper bag and stroller—walk through the station, find the Long Island trains, and get on the one to Patchogue. Before they reached Patchogue, though, they would have to switch trains in a town called Babylon.

Abbie hoped they would make it. She thought it would be a miracle if they reached Patchogue without losing anything—or anyone. She wanted a smooth start to her family's trip. The Rossos were going to spend the entire summer in a rented house right on the beach.

Abbie had never been to a beach for such a long stretch of time. No one in her family had. And that was why her father was driving to Patchogue instead of taking the train. The Rossos' van was loaded with a summer's worth of clothes, toys, and Keegan's baby equipment, plus things that didn't come with the house: sheets, blankets, beach chairs, a small TV, a portable radio, a blender, Zsa-Zsa's litter box, Mrs. Rosso's sewing machine, Mr. Rosso's woodworking tools, and a few other things that Abbie couldn't remember.

Abbie was terribly excited about the summer on the beach. Fire Island sounded so glamorous. Who knew what might happen, whom she might meet. The one bad thing about the summer was that her father could only spend weekends with his family. The rest of the time he would have to be at his job in New York City.

"Poor guy," said Bainbridge, interrupting Abbie's thoughts. He turned to his sister. "I was just thinking about Dad," he explained.

"Me too!" exclaimed Abbie.

"He gets stuck driving the van to Patchogue to meet us at the ferry dock," Bainbridge went on. "He spends this first weekend with us when mostly we'll be cleaning the house and unpacking and putting our stuff away, and then he has to leave on Monday morning to get back to the city—and stay with Uncle Jimmy and Aunt Martha and Scott and Lyman and Courtenay and Eleanor."

Abbie's father held some top-level job at a big, important advertising agency. Normally, he commuted between New York and the Rossos' New Jersey farm. But a daily commute between Fire Island and New York was too long, so he had arranged to live with his brother's family in New York City on weekdays that summer. Abbie felt sorry for him. He didn't get much of a vacation.

"Are we almost there?" Jan asked her mother again. Jan had moved back to her seat next to Ira, her favorite person in the family.

"No," replied Mrs. Rosso. "Why?" she asked suspiciously.

"Because . . . because . . . my tummy doesn't feel good."

Ira leaped out of the seat in a second, ran down the aisle, and squished himself next to Bainbridge, which was as far from Jan as he could get without being in another car. Ira might be a nice older brother, but he was finicky and neat and clean, and didn't want to have a thing to do with Jan if she was going to throw up.

Which she did.

But Mrs. Rosso was prepared. She whipped a plastic bag from among Keegan's supplies and thrust it at Candy who rushed it over to Jan and held it open just in time.

"Oh," groaned Jan when she was finished.

"See? I told you not to ride facing backward," said Candy. (Jan and Ira had gleefully chosen a seat facing Faustine and Dinnie so that the four of them could play games. Faustine and Dinnie had not been nearly so enthusiastic about the arrangement as the younger kids had.) "You always get sick when you ride backward," added Candy.

Bainbridge stood up and slid the back of Jan's seat in the other direction so that she could face forward. Then Jan sat down looking uncomfortable and angry, and Candy held up the barf bag for the whole world to see and said, "What am I supposed to do with *this*?"

Abbie slid down in her seat, wanting to die. She loved her brothers and sisters. She really did.

But this was just too much.

"Take it into the bathroom and dispose of it," Mrs. Rosso replied formally.

"Where's the bathroom?" asked Candy. She was still holding up the bag. It was dangling from between her thumb and forefinger, and Abbie was terrified that she would drop it.

"At the back of the car, near Bainbridge," said Mrs. Rosso, pointing.

Candy walked to the bathroom, holding the bag with one hand and her nose with the other. When she emerged a few moments later, she announced, "Whew, does it ever smell in there—and it wasn't Jan's barf."

Abbie opened a newspaper and tried to hide behind it. Ordinarily, she acted like a mother to the other kids, but on this train full of people, she was hoping no one would know she was part of the Rosso family. She waited until things had died down a little before she put the paper away, sat up straight, and counted heads again.

The trip remained uneventful until just before the train reached Penn Station in New York. Then everything fell apart. First, Abbie realized that her mother was feeding Keegan strained bananas, and the whole car smelled of banana baby food.

Then she noticed that Woody and Hardy were having a terrible time keeping still. They kept jumping up and running down the aisle or asking Mrs. Rosso questions.

Hardy went to the drinking fountain eight times, getting a new paper cone at each visit and using the cones to make horns for his head and ridiculous pointed noses.

Then Abbie realized that the twins were missing. She had to search frantically to find them. They'd secretly moved themselves to the front of the car and were pretending they were French—as if anyone would believe them. Abbie heard snatches of conversation that sounded like this:

"Voo-voo-vay de-jay?"

"Ah, non, non, non. Moi, je-voo-voo de-jay dee touchay le voudoire, non ploo?"

"Ah, oui, but of course. Le voudoire ooh le voodweeze. Comme çi, comme ça. Le pay ay le cacherel. Ça la."

Abbie made a dash for her mother. "Mom," she hissed. "The twins are pretending they're—"

But Mrs. Rosso interrupted her. "Honey, we're just about to reach the station. Would you please make sure nobody forgets anything? And ask Bainbridge to help me with Keegan's stroller."

"Okay," Abbie replied calmly, but her head was spinning. She was certain they were going to lose someone. She made a mental note to take Zsa-Zsa's carrier herself. She was sure that, in the excitement, no one else would remember the cat.

Abbie approached each of her brothers and sisters and said, "Pack up *all* your stuff. We're going to get off soon." Then she remembered to tell Bainbridge to get Keegan's stroller off the overhead rack.

The train jerked to a stop, and suddenly the aisles were crowded with people. Somehow, the Rossos reached their next train on time. They ran through Penn Station, Mrs. Rosso pushing Keegan in his stroller, Abbie holding tightly to Zsa-Zsa's carrier, and the older kids holding onto the younger ones. When they dashed onto the second train, Abbie took yet another head count before anyone even sat down—ten kids, one baby, one mother, one cat, one stroller, and a million tote bags and knapsacks.

They had done it.

The train reached Babylon, and the Rossos made another successful switch onto the last train. Then finally . . . *finally* . . . they pulled into Patchogue.

"Where's Daddy?" asked Ira immediately.

"He's across town at the parking lot for the ferry dock—I hope," replied Mrs. Rosso. "We'll have to take taxis to get there."

"Poo-pay moi le ou-bluh-jay," remarked Faustine.

Abbie rolled her eyes. Then she looked around and saw the line of taxis waiting to drive people to the ferry dock. The Rossos hailed four of them, squeezed inside, and set off on the ten-minute drive through town. When the driver of Abbie's taxi turned the corner to the ferry dock, Abbie immediately noticed two things: one, her father and the van were waiting, and two, it had begun to rain.

"Oh no," said Abbie. "Rain, ugh. But at least Dad's here."

"La, la, la. Une terrible shame," said Dinnie, and Hannah nudged her in the ribs and told her to shut up.

Abbie's cab parked first. Abbie flew out, Zsa-Zsa in hand, paid the driver, and ran to their father.

"We made it!" she announced, holding a sweater over her head to keep the rain off, and peering through the window at Mr. Rosso.

He didn't answer. He was engrossed in a carpentry magazine.

"Dad?" said Abbie.

Mr. Rosso dragged himself away from the magazine. "Yes? . . . Oh, Abbie! You're here!" He leaped out of the van. (Her father was *so* absentminded, thought Abbie.)

"Yup, we made it," she replied. "We didn't lose anyone, and Jan only barfed once. But the twins are doing that French thing again."

Mr. Rosso grinned. Then his smile faded. "It's *raining*!" he exclaimed.

How, Abbie wondered, could her father have sat in a metal van and not have heard the rain?

"It started a few minutes ago," she informed him, "and it looks like it's going to get worse." She glanced at the sky over the bay. It was as black as tar. In the distance she could hear thunder.

"Well, in that case," said her father, "I've got good news and bad news. The bad news is that the ferry doesn't leave for forty-five minutes and there's no waiting room here. The good news is that your mother probably knows exactly where the raincoats are packed."

Abbie nodded grimly as she was surrounded by the other members of her wet family, and the taxis drove off. It turned out that there was more good news and more bad news. The good news was that her mother *did* know exactly where the raincoats were packed. The bad news was that Mr. Rosso would have to unpack the entire van to get to them, and Mrs. Rosso didn't want to unpack until it was time to board the ferry, because of the rain.

In the end, they placed Keegan in the infant seat in the van while the rest of them huddled under a plastic tarp for almost forty-five minutes.

Then the ferry office came to life. In no time at all, the Rossos had bought tickets for the ride to Fire Island, loaded everything from the van into the freight compartment of the ferry, and soon were boarding the boat themselves.

The ferry was named *Kiki* and had seats on top, out in the open, and more seats below, where it was dry.

"We're going to sit on top!" cried Woody, heading for the stairs, followed by Hardy and Hannah.

"In the *rain*?" replied Mrs. Rosso. "Oh no, you're not."

"Les boys eh Hannah son tray, tray bad," whispered Faustine to Dinnie, as Woody, Hardy, and Hannah sat sulkily with the rest of their family.

A few moments later, Abbie felt a bump, then heard the sound of engines starting, and realized that the *Kiki* was pulling away from the dock.

"Good-bye, van," said Mr. Rosso, looking out at the

parking lot. He had paid to leave the van there over the weekend. It had cost a fortune.

Twenty minutes after the ferry had left Patchogue, it arrived at . . . Fire Island! Abbie's family was staying in a little community called Davis Park, which was so close to another community, Ocean Ridge, that you could barely tell where one ended and the other began.

The first thing Abbie said as she emerged from the ferry was "Ooh, look!"

Fire Island was not at all what she had expected. On the bay side, where they had landed, she could see only wooden houses, narrow wooden boardwalks, and, in the middle of the island, trees. Trees? At the beach? And there were no roads or cars, and nothing that even looked like a town.

"On the other side of the island are the beach and the ocean," her father said, as they stood dripping in the rain (except for Keegan who had been zipped inside the plastic cover of his stroller).

It took at least five trips between the ferry and the Rossos' beach house (which was a good walk from the dock) to transport all of their possessions—even with the help of the red wagon that was chained to the porch of the house.

"A wagon!" Hardy exclaimed in dismay. "I'm not pulling one of those around. They're baby toys."

"Not here," Mr. Rosso informed him. "They're like cars. Everyone uses them."

Woody snorted. Then he went off to explore the house.

Abbie explored it, too, once she'd helped out with some of the unpacking. It was a huge house, as Davis Park houses seemed to go. And it was set on a stretch of beach which looked deserted, but that might have been due to the rain.

"Maybe we'll have the beach to ourselves all summer!" said Candy.

Abbie hoped not. She wanted to meet some new people.

She was about to leave the living room, with its view of the ocean, to see what the kitchen was like, when suddenly Candy gasped.

"What is it?" asked Abbie, alarmed.

"Look at the house next door!"

Abbie looked out a side window at the rundown, ramshackle house. It was obvious that no one had lived in it for years. "So?" she said.

"It's haunted," whispered Candy. "It must be."

"Oh, for heaven's sake," said Abbie. Suddenly she had had enough of her family. Besides, the rain had stopped.

"Mom, can I walk around outside for a while?" she asked.

"Have you unpacked your clothes?" asked Mrs. Rosso.

"Yes," replied Abbie, who was sharing a room with

her French twin sisters, which was another reason she needed to get out. She couldn't stand to hear one more "za-zoo" or "oo-vray."

"Okay, go ahead," said Mrs. Rosso.

Abbie let herself out the front door of the house, over which, she noted, hung a sign that read "Sandpiper." All of the houses seemed to be named. She had discovered that on the Rossos' many trips to and from the ferry earlier.

Abbie reached the end of the walk leading to her house, turned onto another, wider boardwalk, continued along it until she reached an intersection overhung with trees—and bumped smack into some kids who were laughing and talking on the adjacent boardwalk. The three of them, two girls and a boy, were about her age, and the boy looked awfully familiar.

"Sorry!" exclaimed Abbie. "I couldn't see you."

"That's okay," replied one of the girls with a smile. "It happens all the time at this corner. They need to cut these trees back a little."

The three kids were about to go on when Abbie asked, "Am I heading in the right direction for the Harbor Store?" She knew she wasn't, but she wanted to talk for a few moments longer. She wanted to figure out why the boy looked so familiar.

And then the boy opened his mouth. "As a matter of fact, you're not," he told her. That was all he had to say for Abbie to realize who he was. He wasn't just any boy. He was a movie star. He was *Justin Hart*.

Abbie's mouth dropped open. She couldn't help it. Justin was the star of a hit TV series, and he'd made several big movies.

The girls grinned. "You just recognized him, right?" said one.

Abbie nodded. She couldn't say a word.

"Well, you can talk to him," the girl went on. "He's just a regular guy. Also, he's my boyfriend. I'm Melanie Braderman. You know Justin, I guess, and this is my friend Lacey Reeder."

Lacey, who looked gorgeous and sophisticated to Abbie, smiled too. "Are you here for the summer?" she asked.

Abbie nodded again. Then she managed to say, "This is our first time here. We live in New Jersey. But we used to live in New York City."

"Really?" said Lacey. "That's where I live!"

Abbie stood and talked with Melanie, Lacey, and Justin. The longer they talked, the more relaxed Abbie felt, and the more Justin really did seem like just a regular guy. It turned out that the Bradermans and the Reeders had summered in Davis Park practically forever and that Melanie had met Justin there shortly before he became a star. Now Justin was back to shoot a movie—right in Davis Park! He and his camera crew and the other actors and actresses would be there most of the summer.

Abbie showed Melanie, Lacey, and Justin where Sandpiper House was and made plans to meet them on the beach the next day. Then she went home—happily. She'd been on Fire Island for just two and a half hours, and already she'd made three friends.

She belonged.

2

Calandra and the Mystery Next Door

Candy woke up slowly the next morning. She was the kind of person who liked to savor things—books, warm breezes, good smells, and the feel of a soft bed in the early morning.

It was the beginning of the Rossos' first full day at Sandpiper House. Candy yawned and stretched and looked around her room. It was the tiniest bedroom in the house, which was why she had chosen it for herself. Of all of the Rosso kids, Candy craved solitude and privacy the most, and this little bedroom could sleep only one person. The house as a whole, like a lot of houses in Davis Park, could sleep an army. The beach houses had plenty of rooms. And in each bedroom were two or three beds or sometimes even bunk beds. The couches in the living room were usually designed for sleeping, too. All of this was because people with houses on Fire Island liked to invite guests for visits.

The day before, when the Rosso kids were running around counting bedrooms and figuring out who would share with whom, Candy had found this tiny room and begged to have it for herself. Her brothers and sisters had let her. They knew Candy needed privacy. And so Keegan and Mr. and Mrs. Rosso had wound up in one bedroom—not even the biggest, since Mr. Rosso would be at Sandpiper House only on the weekends—Abbie and the twins were sharing another (the twins in bunk beds); Bainbridge and Woody were sharing the fourth bedroom; Hardy and Ira, the fifth; and Jan and Hannah, the sixth.

These last two sets of roommates were not ideal. Jan and Ira wanted desperately to share a room, but Hannah flat-out refused to share with Hardy, so the younger kids had to make do. Candy felt a *little* selfish about getting her own room, but she knew it would be the best summer of her life. She'd probably never have so much privacy again.

On that first morning in Sandpiper House, Candy was lying in bed savoring things. Her window was open slightly, and although the shade was drawn, she could smell salt water and hear the ocean beating against the shore. A moment later, she heard a gull cry, then the leaves of the trees rustling. A perfect morning.

Candy got out of bed slowly. She padded barefoot

across the room to the window, pulled up the shade, and found herself looking directly into a window of the rundown house next door. It was a typical beach house, built on stilts in case the ocean water ever came far enough up the beach to reach the house. A boardwalk led to the front door, and a railing ran around the weathered, gray deck of the house. But the house, which didn't seem to have a name, was not nearly as nice-looking as Sandpiper House. Boards were missing here and there in the walk, a railing was leaning dangerously to one side, and several of the windows were cracked. But not the window Candy was looking into. It was intact. There were even ratty curtains hanging in it, and when Candy snapped up her shade, she thought she saw one of the curtains flutter slightly.

Candy gasped.

Was someone in the house? Someone must be! What else would make a curtain move—an inside curtain in a closed-up house?

Then a chilling thought came to Candy. Someone must be in that awful house. She didn't know if the person were living or dead—a human or a ghost—but someone must be there.

Candy pulled her shade down again. She waited for three minutes (timing it on her stopwatch). Then she snapped up the shade again.

Nothing.

The curtains were not stirring.

Maybe Candy had imagined the curtain moving.

She did have a good imagination, and she liked mysteries. She decided to keep this mystery to herself, at least for awhile. It would be something else to savor.

Candy changed into her bathing suit and put a T-shirt on over it. Then she sauntered into the kitchen area, where she found her mother feeding Keegan and her father reading his carpentry magazine.

"Morning, early bird," Mrs. Rosso greeted her.

"Morning," Candy replied.

"Ready for the beach?" asked Mr. Rosso, dragging himself away from his magazine.

"Yup," replied Candy. Then she said, "Think of it. A *whole summer* of sand and sun and swimming." She paused. Then she added, "Maybe since we *do* have a whole summer of sand and sun and swimming, I won't go to the beach today after all. Maybe I'll just walk around Davis Park and see what's what."

Mr. Rosso nodded. "Check out the store? Go to the boat dock?"

"Yes," answered Candy, even though that wasn't what she meant at all. She was thinking about her mystery and how to solve it. She supposed she could ask people about the strange house. Or she could just walk up to the front door, knock a couple of times, and see if anyone answered. Of course, if no one did, it wouldn't mean a thing. If someone lived there, he or she might be out jogging or at the grocery store or something.

Candy couldn't decide what to do. By the time the

rest of her brothers and sisters had gotten up, she was just sitting in the living room, looking out the window at the ramshackle house. She had thought about spying on it for the entire day but had discarded the idea. Her mother might think she was sick if she didn't leave the house.

Candy was thinking up another plan when Abbie said to her, "Hey, Candy, you know those three kids I met yesterday?"

Of course Candy knew. By then, all of the Rossos knew about Justin Hart and his friends. They couldn't believe that Abbie had met a celebrity and was going to spend the day with him.

"Yeah?" replied Candy.

"Well, I'm going to watch him shoot a scene on the beach this morning. Melanie and Lacey will be there, too. Want to come with us?"

Candy had a funny feeling that her sister felt sorry for her because she was just sitting there, staring out the window. But she was not going to pass up the opportunity to meet Justin Hart or at least to watch him work.

"Sure!" exclaimed Candy. She was also pleased that her big sister was going to include her in an activity with her new friends. Not that she and Abbie didn't get along; it was just that Candy was flattered when her older sister offered to include her.

Candy resolved then and there to act as grown-up

and as sophisticated as Abbie. She didn't want to let her sister down.

Near ten o'clock, Abbie said, "Ready to go, Candy? I'm supposed to meet Mel and Lacey now."

"Yup, I'm ready," replied Candy. She was glad that, at least on this first day, her other sisters and brothers were too eager to explore the island or do beach things rather than spend the morning hanging around a movie star. Bainbridge was already settled on a chair on the Rossos' deck, facing the ocean with a pair of binoculars. He said he was "chick-watching," which Abbie told him was a sexist comment. Jan and Ira were in the ocean under the watchful eye of Mr. Rosso. The twins, the nature-lovers in the family, had decided to walk through the wildlife sanctuary, and Hardy, Woody, and Hannah were going to walk with them and then go on to a place called Watch Hill where, they'd heard, there was a snack bar that served pizza. (Mrs. Rosso was still organizing the beach house. It was a big job, but Keegan took long naps, and Mrs. Rosso loved to organize, so that was a fine arrangement.)

Candy set off proudly with her older sister.

"Where are we going to meet your friends?" she asked.

"A little farther down the beach, where it's *really* deserted. That's where they're shooting today's scene."

"What's the movie about?" asked Candy.

"I'm not sure," replied Abbie. "We'll find out when we get there."

They didn't have to walk far. From the front of Sandpiper House, Candy could see all of the movie equipment down the beach—trailers and tents and cameras and directors' chairs and lots of people. How had the trailers gotten across the bay to the island? Candy wondered. Oh well. Movie people had ways of getting things done.

When Candy and her sister reached the site of the shoot, Candy turned around to see how far they'd walked. She could see Sandpiper House clearly and the house next door even more clearly, since it was closer. She thought she could see her father and Jan and Ira, but she wasn't sure.

Candy paused to enjoy that particular moment. There she was on the set of a movie and on the beach, too. The morning sun was growing hot, and it warmed her shoulders. She thought about taking her T-shirt off, but no one on the set except Justin Hart was wearing only a bathing suit. Everyone else was either dressed or was wearing a cover-up over his bathing suit. Candy sank her toes into the warm sand and wiggled them down until she reached the damp, cool sand underneath. A small wave rolled in and lapped at her ankles.

"Candy? Hey, Candy!"

Abbie was calling her. Candy looked up. She pulled her feet out of the sand. Abbie was standing nearby with two girls, a thin, dark-haired one and a blonde, sophisticated-looking one. Candy ran to them.

"You guys," said Abbie to the girls, "this is my sister Candy."

"Hi," said Candy. "My real name's Calandra." Lately, she felt she had to say that. Candy was a nice enough name, but it was sort of babyish.

"Hello," the dark-haired girl replied. "I'm Melanie Braderman. Most people call me Mel."

"And I'm Lacey Reeder," said the other girl. "Most people call me Lacey."

Everyone laughed.

"How do you like Fire Island so far?" Mel asked Candy.

"It's great. I have my own room."

"Well, in that huge house, I'd think so," said Lacey.

Candy and Abbie looked at each other. For some reason, it was hard for them to tell people about the size of their family. Bainbridge never had any trouble with it. He never had any trouble telling people his name, either. He'd come right out and say that he was Bainbridge and he had ten brothers and sisters, a mother with a system for everything from folding clothes to naming her kids, and an amazingly absent-minded father.

Abbie cleared her throat. "Well," she said to her new friends, "the house is big, but not for us. There are thirteen people in our family."

"Plus Zsa-Zsa," added Candy. "She's our cat."

"Thirteen people!" exclaimed Lacey. "Wow. Mel and I only have five people in our families."

"Yeah," agreed Mel. "We each have our parents, a stuck-up older sister, and a pesty younger brother." She paused. "So you've got *ten* brothers and sisters?" she said to Abbie.

Abbie nodded. Then she began the countdown, and Candy could feel her face flush.

"There's me, I'm the oldest. Then there're Bainbridge, Calandra, Dagwood, Eberhard, Faustine and Gardenia—they're twins—Hannah, Ira, Janthina, and Keegan. Keegan's the baby."

Candy caught the amazed expressions on the faces of Mel and Lacey. She looked down at her feet. She hoped her sister wasn't going to start in on the explanation of *how* the kids had been named.

But if Abbie was, she didn't have a chance because at that moment an absolutely gorgeous boy walked over to them. Candy knew right away that he was Justin Hart, America's Hart-throb. She couldn't believe she was seeing him in person. He looked much, much cuter in real life than he did on TV or on the movie screen. His brown eyes were wide set, a few freckles were scattered over his nose, his legs were *long*, and he grinned at Candy from under a mop of dark curls.

"You've got to be Abbie's sister," he said. "You two look so much alike. It's unbelievable. How old are you?"

"Thirteen," Candy mumbled. She felt terribly shy. What had happened to her resolve to act grown-up in front of Abbie? She might as well have stuck her head in the sand.

But Abbie took over. "We all look alike," she told Justin. "There are eleven of us. Kids, I mean, and we all have brown hair and freckles."

"*Eleven?*" cried Justin, and Abbie had to explain about their family again.

"Justin?" a voice boomed a few minutes later.

"I'm wanted on the set," said Justin with a grin, and he ran over to talk to three men while a woman combed his hair and another one rubbed something from a jar across his cheeks.

Candy had almost forgotten that a movie was being shot just ten feet away from her. Suddenly, she found her voice. "What's the movie about?" she asked Mel.

"Oh, it's going to be really fun. It's called *Summer Blues*, and it's about this boy, played by Justin, who goes to Fire Island for the summer while his parents are getting divorced. His family is really rich, and they rent this huge old house, and his mom and dad take turns coming out to stay with him and his house-keeper. Meanwhile, Justin is trying to get his parents back together, plus he gets caught between two girls— one who has a crush on him but whom he doesn't like much, and another whom he loves but who has a crush on a boy that Justin has gotten to be friends with."

"Oh," said Candy. "It does sound fun—but complicated."

"It's supposed to be complicated," said Mel. "That's part of what makes it a good movie. I mean, not *too* complicated, but you have to have a plot and some subplots and stuff."

Candy nodded. She knew about those things. She loved to read. She guessed that if you needed plots and subplots in books, you needed them in movies, too. A movie was just another way of telling a story.

"You should see the things the special effects people can do," Mel went on. "They're really amazing. See that trailer over there? That's where the equipment is kept. And see that man and woman? The ones talking to Justin now? They're Nate and Maxie, and they can do almost anything. They can make lightning flash—I mean, not really. It just looks like it—"

"And they can make the weirdest, scariest sounds," Lacey added, just as someone shouted, "Places, everyone!"

The shooting of the scene was about to begin. For the next hour or so, the movie crew worked hard. Candy was surprised at how often Justin and the other actors had to say their lines. Sometimes they said them over and over and over before the director decided they were just right.

Candy was interested at first, but after a while her attention began to wander. She gazed behind her at the rundown old house. She couldn't stop looking at it and wondering about it. When the director finally called for a break, Candy said to Mel, "You know the house next door to ours?"

Mel looked where Candy was pointing. "Yeah?" she said.

"How old is it? Does anyone live there?"

"How old?" Mel repeated. "Gosh, I'm not sure. It can't be too old. This community isn't very old. I bet it's maybe fifty years."

"At most," spoke up Lacey, who'd been listening. "Probably a lot less."

"And no one lives there," said Mel. "It's been deserted for as long as my parents have been spending the summers here, which is about twenty years now. I don't even remember—"

"Places, everyone!" yelled the director again.

Abbie, Mel, and Lacey turned to watch Justin in action, but Candy couldn't take her eyes off the old house. She felt drawn to it.

That night, Candy lay alone in her tiny bedroom. The time was three-thirty. She'd been asleep, but something had woken her up.

It was moaning.

Candy listened. She could no longer hear it. But she was sure she'd heard it earlier. She wanted to go to her parents and tell them about it, but at dinner that night she'd said something about the weird house next door, and her parents had said her imagination was running away with her. Furthermore, Hannah had snorted and called Candy a dweeb, which caused Hannah to be sent from the table without dessert.

Now Candy didn't care what Hannah or anyone else thought. She heard the moaning again, and she knew it was coming from the house. When she worked up the nerve to tiptoe to the window, the moaning became louder.

The next night, she thought she heard rain, which was a lovely nighttime sound, but when she awoke in the morning, the island was dry—except for Candy's windowsill and the deck beneath it.

Three nights later, Candy's nightmares began. They were terrifying and vivid, as if they were really happening to her, and she dreamed two of them several times over.

In one dream, Candy was way out in the ocean all by herself. The sky was very dark. She couldn't tell if that was because it was night or because a storm was brewing. At first, Candy seemed to be in some sort of boat or maybe on a raft. Then suddenly the waves swelled, and the wind blew, and nothing was supporting Candy anymore. She was being sucked down into the black ocean, and water was in her ears, her nose, her mouth, filling up her lungs.

She couldn't breathe! She was drowning.

Then her eyes would fly open, and she would lie on her back, gasping, as if she'd just come to the surface of the ocean and had finally reached air.

The other nightmare wasn't quite so frightening, but it was eerie. The dream would start off in a grassy place. At first, Candy felt at peace, even though the day was gray and dreary, and her shoes and feet were wet. Then Candy would realize that the grassy place wasn't just a hillside but also a graveyard. All around her were once-white tombstones turning gray with age. And *then* she would realize that she wasn't alone. People were starting to trickle into the cemetery. Candy noticed that they were wearing black, even the children. She looked down and saw that she was wearing black, too. Most of the people were moaning and crying, and they were walking slowly through the cemetery to a spot where two graves had been dug. Candy followed the people and saw that one grave was big, and beside it sat a dark adult-size coffin. The other grave was small, and beside it sat a white child-size coffin. A priest said a blessing, the caskets were lowered into the ground, and then everyone and everything around Candy just faded away until she was left standing in nothingness.

And that was when she would wake up from the second dream.

*   *   *

After Candy had had the dreams several times, a gnawing sense of terror began to overcome her each night, but it would disappear during the day. In the sunshine, with the sand and the beach and her family around, she could forget about the nightmares—but not about the house.

Candy was certain now that the house was haunted. She had developed her own theory about how it got that way, and why, as a result, no one ever rented it. The haunting also explained why Candy heard moaning and saw odd things inside the house. But why did the ghosts make rain at her window? Why did they give her bad dreams? And most of all, why were they picking on Candy?

Candy had read that spirits and poltergeists sometimes haunted young people, like in that scary movie in which the girl is possessed by the devil. But Candy wasn't the only young teenager in her family. What about Bainbridge? Or Woody? Woody was going to turn thirteen soon. Candy thought someone who was almost thirteen ought to be the perfect target for a ghost. But nobody else was complaining of strange occurrences or dreams. And every time Candy did, her brothers and sisters teased her.

Candy learned not to open her mouth and to keep to herself. She usually hung around alone anyway. And she decided that if she did only one important thing that summer, it would be to solve the mystery of the house next door. She would do it if it killed her, which she sincerely hoped it wouldn't. And then she could show everyone in her family that she wasn't crazy after all, and that there *are* mysterious things in the world, things that can't be explained naturally. . . .

3

Faustine and the Great Fish Protest

Faustine and her twin sister Gardenia loved animals and nature. They loved them more than anyone in their family did, and they knew a lot about every creature in the animal kingdom, from ants to elephants. They were the only ones who'd been truly excited to learn that Fire Island was a national seashore (like a national park, except that it was a beach).

One morning Faustine decided to get up early and do some birdwatching from the Rossos' deck. There were all kinds of birds in the shrubbery and trees around Sandpiper House. Faustine had seen catbirds, swallows, sparrows, turtledoves, mockingbirds, orioles, and more. They were active throughout the day, but they were especially active (and noisy) in the morning.

So, before anyone else in Sandpiper House—even Dinnie—was awake, Faustine was sitting at the picnic table on the back deck. A doughnut was in front of her on a napkin, but she hadn't taken a bite yet. She was holding a pair of binoculars to her eyes and watching two swallows on the branch of a tree. She'd also been watching a rabbit, a young one, that she was pretty sure lived under their house.

Suddenly the back door banged open and shut, scattering the birds and the rabbit. The peaceful morning was ruined.

"Let me have those!" exclaimed Candy, grabbing the binoculars from Faustine. The binoculars were on a strap around Faustine's neck, and Candy practically strangled her.

"What's wrong?" asked Faustine in a loud whisper, not wanting to wake up everyone else. She glared at her sister, who was already dressed in her bathing suit. So was Faustine, for that matter. The Rossos rarely bothered with actual clothes on Fire Island, except for Ira because he burned so easily.

Candy ran around to one of the side decks with the binoculars. She peered at the rundown house next door, muttering something about a ghost. Faustine just shrugged. Ever since the Rossos first reached Fire Island, Candy had been obsessed with the house next door.

Since it was still early, Faustine decided to take a

walk on the beach. She wanted to see who else would be out at that hour. So she picked up her doughnut, ran to the beach, and soon discovered who the other early risers were—joggers, dog walkers, and fishermen.

Three fishermen were set up just a little distance from Sandpiper House. One of them was seated on a canvas folding chair without a back. The other two were standing up. The one who was seated had stuck his pole in the sand beside him. He wasn't even holding onto it. He was just sitting and waiting for the fish to bite. The other men kept casting their lines into the ocean, then slowly reeling them back. At the feet of each of the three sat a tackle box.

Faustine decided that the fisherman who was sitting down was very lazy. He would never catch any fish that way.

Her hands behind her back, the doughnut half-eaten, Faustine watched the men for a long time. She watched the two who were standing up reel their lines in, fiddle with their tackle boxes, change the lures, and cast over and over again.

Suddenly, the fisherman who was sitting down jumped to his feet and cried, "I got one! I got something big!"

Faustine's eyes grew wide. She took a step closer to the man as he pulled his pole out of the sand, leaned back, and started jerkily reeling in his line. It looked like very hard work. Several times, the man shouted, "I'm losing him! I'm losing him!" But he landed the fish without any real problem.

Faustine peered at the fish. The hook was still stuck in his mouth. She watched as the fisherman grasped the fish around the middle and yanked the hook out of his mouth. The fish flip-flopped back and forth, back and forth. He looked afraid and unhappy. Then the man placed the fish beside his chair, and the fish lay in the sand, his mouth opening and closing. He looked as if he were gasping for breath, even though Faustine knew full well that fish breathe through gills. Finally, the fish lay still.

Faustine realized that she had just watched a living thing die. She knew, of course, that fish die after they've been caught, but she'd never seen it happen. Did it have to take so long? The man caught the fish, then tossed him to the sand and let him die slowly. That was not humane.

Faustine turned and ran back to Sandpiper House. Somewhere along the way, she dropped the uneaten part of her doughnut, but she didn't care. She had to tell Dinnie what the fishermen were doing.

When she reached the house, she tore up the stairs. She almost yelled out, "Dinnie! Binkle-rod!" That meant "Emergency!" The twins had their own private language—they'd used it ever since they'd started talking—but they rarely used it anymore.

They had decided they were too grown-up for it. Faustine ran into the bedroom she was sharing with her sisters, shook Dinnie on the shoulder, and said, "Dinnie! Emergency! You have to come to the beach *right now*!"

Dinnie was barely awake, but she recognized the tone of her twin's voice. It meant, *There really is trouble*. So she threw off her covers and leaped out of bed.

Faustine was relieved to see that Dinnie had slept in her bathing suit. Good. They wouldn't have to waste a second.

The girls raced back to the beach. Faustine pulled Dinnie to where the fishermen were still fishing away. Just as the girls arrived, one of the men who was standing up reeled in a fish. Faustine saw that the three of them had now caught several fish.

"Watch. Just watch," she said to Dinnie.

Dinnie watched. She saw the same flip-flopping and gasping that Faustine had seen, and then, after what seemed like an eternity, the fish lay still. Dead.

"That's horrible!" cried Dinnie. "Why did you make me come down here to see that?" she demanded.

"Because we have to do something to stop those men," Faustine replied. "They shouldn't be allowed to kill fish that way."

"What should we do?"

"Tell them to cut it out."

Dinnie looked skeptical. "I don't know . . ."

"Oh, come on," said Faustine, even though she was usually shy about approaching people she didn't know and asking them for favors.

"All right," replied Dinnie. She took a step forward, then stopped.

"What's wrong?" asked Faustine.

"Nothing. I just had an idea. Let me talk first, okay?"

"Okay," replied Faustine.

The girls walked to the lazy fisherman who was sitting down.

"Good morning," said Dinnie pleasantly.

"Morning," replied the man, glancing up at the twins, surprised.

"That's a pretty big fish you caught," said Dinnie, pointing to the one Faustine had watched die.

"Sure is."

"You must have worked hard to catch him," Dinnie went on.

"Yup."

"How did you kill him?" asked Dinnie.

The man was beginning to look slightly impatient. "Huh?" he said.

"I asked how you killed him."

The man didn't seem to be paying attention any longer. He looked out toward the sea, watching his line for jerky movements.

"Mister," Dinnie said in a louder voice, "don't you

know it's wrong to catch a living thing and then just put it aside so it will die?"

The man shrugged.

Dinnie decided to give up. She guessed the man had a right to fish if he wanted to.

But Faustine was angry. "Come on!" she cried. She ran to the other two fishermen, the ones who were standing up. She and Dinnie positioned themselves between them. The men were smiling. They'd already overheard the twins talking to their friend.

"Hey!" said Faustine. "Stop this! Stop this right now! You've got to quit being mean to the fish."

"Aw, cheer up, kid," said one of the men. "This is legal. Completely legal. And the fish never feel a thing."

"I'll bet," muttered Faustine.

"This is our sport," said the third fisherman. "We come here every morning, don't we?" he said, looking at his friends.

"Sure do," replied the lazy one.

"Your sport? You mean you kill the fish just for fun?" exploded Faustine.

"Naw, we eat them."

Faustine let out the breath she'd been holding. She couldn't win. She took one last look at the dead fish lying on the beach. "Matter-barn," she said to Dinnie, forgetting that she was too old to use their private language. ("Matter-barn" meant "Okay, I give up.")

Sadly, the twins walked back to Sandpiper House.

But Faustine didn't give up. She knew there were things she could do, things that would make a difference to all of the animals in the world that were being killed cruelly by human beings.

At dinner that night she ate salad, corn on the cob, and bread, but when Mrs. Rosso offered her a piece of steak, Faustine said politely, "No, thank you."

"No?" Mrs. Rosso raised her eyebrows. "You need your protein," she said.

Faustine replied, "Thanks, but I would rather not eat a dead animal. I have no idea how it was killed."

At breakfast the next morning, Faustine ate half a grapefruit and two pieces of toast and drank a glass of orange juice. But she would not eat the scrambled eggs that Abbie had prepared.

"*They're* not dead animals," Abbie pointed out.

"Are too," Faustine countered stubbornly, even though she wasn't sure.

That was on Wednesday. By Friday, Faustine would eat only fruits, vegetables, pasta, and bread. She wouldn't even drink milk.

"Why not?" demanded Mrs. Rosso, sounding horribly exasperated.

"Because milk comes from cows, and it's cruel to milk cows with machines." Mrs. Rosso rolled her eyes upward.

"Hey, Faustine," said Hannah tauntingly, "guess what else is made with milk. Milk chocolate. You'll have to give up candy, too."

Faustine loved candy. But if she had to give it up, then she would give it up.

By Friday night when Mr. Rosso arrived on the island for the weekend, he found his entire family fed up with Faustine.

"Dad, she's driving us crazy," said Bainbridge. "She makes us feel guilty every time we put a piece of meat in our mouths. She gives us these *looks*, like we're practically cannibals."

Mr. Rosso smiled, but later that night he fixed a turkey sandwich as a snack and received one of Faustine's *looks* himself.

"Faustine," said Mr. Rosso, purposely taking a huge bite of the sandwich.

"What?" she replied. They were sitting on the deck overlooking the ocean. The outdoor lights were on, and Faustine had propped her feet up on one of the railings.

"Do you know what the food chain is?"

"No." Faustine squirmed in her chair. She had a feeling her father was going to say something she didn't want to hear.

"In the animal world," began Mr. Rosso, "and let me remind you that humans are animals too, littler or weaker animals are eaten by bigger or stronger animals. That's the law of nature. That's how all animals, including humans, have survived since the world began."

"But we don't need to eat animals."

"No, *we* don't need to, but some people still survive on animals. Furthermore, if we never killed another animal, the world would be overrun with them. There's a town in New Jersey that has a terrible problem with deer. They wander up and down the streets and through yards. They eat people's gardens and plants because there isn't enough food in the woods for all of them anymore."

"Oh," said Faustine. She thought that over. Then she said, "But there are humane ways to kill animals and there are cruel ways. Also, I don't think it's fair to kill animals for fun."

"No," agreed Mr. Rosso. "I don't think so either, but I do think it's okay to kill animals for food. I can only hope they are killed humanely. Faustine, you may eat whatever you want, as long as your diet is balanced and healthy, okay? No one will expect you to eat meat or fish."

"Okay."

"But I want you to realize two things. One, not everyone in this family agrees with your views, and they'll be much happier if you stop giving them a hard time. Two, we get a lot more from animals than food. If I were you, I'd take off your sandals."

"Why?" asked Faustine.

"Because they're leather. They're made from animal hide."

Faustine sat up and yanked her sandals off. She never wore them again.

The next morning, Faustine ate fruit and cereal for breakfast. When she turned down milk, no one asked her why, and Faustine didn't lecture her brothers and sisters about milking machines—although she wanted to. But there was one thing Faustine could do, and she talked to Dinnie about her idea. Then she and her twin found some plywood boards on the beach. Using fat black Magic Markers, they made signs that read: "No Fishing," "Fishing Is Cruel," and "Boycott Fish." The twins stuck them in the sand near the fishermen. But the signs didn't stop the men from fishing.

In fact, the signs made them mad. Each time the girls stuck a sign in the sand, one of the men would march over to it and uproot it. Later, when he was done fishing, he would throw it away somewhere.

This happened three mornings in a row. On the fourth morning, the man who fished sitting down waited until Faustine put up a sign that read "Fish Have Feelings Too." He pulled it up immediately. But he didn't take it back to his chair. Instead he marched down the beach with it. He was headed for Sandpiper House.

"What are you doing?" Faustine yelled after him. She glanced at her sister. Then she and Dinnie ran as fast as their legs could carry them. They reached Sandpiper House just as the fisherman did.

"Mom! Mom!" called Faustine, pushing past the man.

"What is it?" replied Mrs. Rosso. She opened the door. Then she caught sight of the fisherman and the sign.

"Excuse me," said the man politely. He removed his hat. He told Mrs. Rosso what the twins had been doing the past few mornings.

Mrs. Rosso listened patiently. Then she asked the twins to apologize to the fisherman. When they had finished, and when they had promised that they wouldn't put up any more signs or bother the fishermen in any way, the man left.

"Faustine," said Mrs. Ro[sso] . . .

ready spoken t[o] . . .

when t[heir] views differ from . . .

have be[en] clearer. M . . .

not to gi . . .

the fisher . . .

Are Pests . . .

"Embar[r] . . .

"So will . . .

rest?"

Faustine n . . .

---

walk on the beach. She wanted to see who else would be out at that hour. So she picked up her doughnut, ran to the beach, and soon discovered who the other early risers were—joggers, dog walkers, and fishermen.

Three fishermen were set up just a little distance from Sandpiper House. One of them was seated on a canvas folding chair without a back. The other two were standing up. The one who was seated had stuck his pole in the sand beside him. He wasn't even holding onto it. He was just sitting and waiting for the fish to bite. The other men kept casting their lines into the ocean, then slowly reeling them back. At the feet of each of the three sat a tackle box.

Faustine decided that the fisherman who was sitting down was very lazy. He would never catch any fish that way.

Her hands behind her back, the doughnut half-eaten, Faustine watched the men for a long time. She watched the two who were standing up reel their lines in, fiddle with their tackle boxes, change the lures, and cast over and over again.

Suddenly, the fisherman who was sitting down jumped to his feet and cried, "I got one! I got something big!"

Faustine's eyes grew wide. She took a step closer to the man as he pulled his pole out of the sand, leaned back, and started jerkily reeling in his line. It looked

So, before anyone else in Sandpiper House—even Dinnie—was awake, Faustine was sitting at the picnic table on the back deck. A doughnut was in front of her on a napkin, but she hadn't taken a bite yet. She was holding a pair of binoculars to her eyes and watching two swallows on the branch of a tree. She'd also been watching a rabbit, a young one, that she was pretty sure lived under their house.

Suddenly the back door banged open and shut, scattering the birds and the rabbit. The peaceful morning was ruined.

"Let me have those!" exclaimed Candy, grabbing the binoculars from Faustine. The binoculars were on a strap around Faustine's neck, and Candy practically strangled her.

"What's wrong?" asked Faustine in a loud whisper, not wanting to wake up everyone else. She glared at her sister, who was already dressed in her bathing suit. So was Faustine, for that matter. The Rossos rarely bothered with actual clothes on Fly Island, except for

Eleven Kids, One Summer
And she did give it a rest. But for the rest of the summer, whenever she took an early morning walk, she turned left instead of right when she reached the beach so that she wouldn't have to walk by the fishermen.

4

Hannah and the Ghosts

It wasn't fair, Hannah thought. It just wasn't fair. Here she was in a family with ten brothers and sisters, and she didn't fit in anywhere. She had no special brother or sister who was her best friend. Jan and Ira had each other, the twins had each other, and Woody and Hardy had each other. Also, she was too young to play with Abbie, Candy, or Bainbridge. Besides, she wasn't interested in the things that interested them. Abbie liked talking about boys, Bainbridge liked girls, and Candy . . . well, Hannah wasn't sure what Candy liked. Candy's head was in the clouds. She was always daydreaming or reading. It was hard to get into her world. Mrs. Rosso said that Candy was romantic, which Hannah thought was even worse then liking boys. Besides, Candy was acting weird that summer.

(Weird for Candy.) She spent more time gazing at the house next door than at the beach.

So that left Keegan. And he was just a baby. What do you do with a baby?

This summer, thought Hannah, is royally boring. It needs to be a little livelier.

Hannah looked for ways to spice up the summer. She tried spying on her brothers and sisters, but Candy caught her, and anyway she couldn't find much that was worth spying on. She tried teaching herself magic from a book, but no one seemed interested in watching card tricks.

What Hannah needed was a friend, but she didn't know how to go about finding one. So she asked herself a question: When I'm at home in New Jersey and I get bored, what do I do?

The answer came to her immediately. She played practical jokes. Well, she could play jokes at the beach just as easily as she could on the farm. (Actually, she had already played a few small jokes on Candy. Now, though, she would become a serious joke-player.)

Hannah's idea came to her late one morning, just before lunchtime. She decided to get to work on it right away.

"Mom?" said Hannah. "I'll set the table for you."

"Thank you," replied Mrs. Rosso, looking surprised. "That will give me a chance to change Keegan. I can smell him from over here."

Hannah worked quickly. Her first joke was so simple it scared her. She dumped the sugar out of the sugar bowl and back into the bag of sugar. Then she filled the empty bowl with salt. When that was done, she quickly set the table. No one would have any idea what she'd done—at first.

But her brothers and sisters found out when they returned to the house for lunch, eagerly poured iced tea from the pitcher into their glasses, and began spooning in salt from the sugar bowl.

Jan was the first to take a drink. She was thirsty from having played on the beach all morning. She took a big gulp—and spat her iced tea across the table at Ira.

"Ew!" they both cried.

"Jan!" exclaimed Mrs. Rosso. "What has gotten into you?"

"There's something wrong with the iced tea!" Jan managed to gasp. "What did you put in it?"

"Tea bags, water, and ice," replied Mrs. Rosso.

Abbie took a swallow of her tea. She grimaced and said, "Um, Mom, Jan's right. This tastes funny."

Woody took a sip. "Funny!" he exclaimed. "It tastes like dog barf!"

"Enough, Woody," said Mrs. Rosso. She tasted the iced tea in the pitcher. "This seems fine to me," she said. Then she tasted the tea in her glass. "Ugh. Something happened to the tea between the pitcher and our glasses."

Woody, who liked to solve mysteries, looked suspiciously at the sugar bowl. He reached for it, wet his finger, stuck it in the bowl ("Ew!" cried finicky Ira again. "Germs!"), and tasted his finger.

"Hey! This is salt, not sugar!" he cried.

At that point, Hannah couldn't help it. She burst out laughing.

"Hannah!" exclaimed Mrs. Rosso. "Is that why you wanted to set the table?"

"Yes!" replied Hannah, giggling helplessly.

For a moment, no one knew whether to scold Hannah or laugh with her. Then all at the same time, the Rossos began to laugh.

That evening, after dinner, Hannah short-sheeted Jan's bed.

"I think I'll go to bed early," she announced afterward. It was only seven-thirty, long before Hannah's summer bedtime, but she wanted to be in the room when Jan climbed into bed.

"Are you feeling all right?" Mrs. Rosso asked Hannah.

"Fine, Mom. I just want to rest up for tomorrow. It's going to be a busy day."

Mrs. Rosso looked skeptical but kissed Hannah good night. Then Hannah went to the room she shared with Jan, got into bed, and waited.

Half an hour later, Jan, already in her pajamas, pulled back the covers on her bed. She climbed in.

Hannah heard her rustling around and smothered a giggle.

"Hey!" cried Jan finally. *"Hey!"*

"What's wrong?" Hannah asked, pretending to sound sleepy.

"Something's the matter with my bed," replied Jan.

"What?" asked Hannah.

"I don't know. I can't see." Jan flicked on the light. She examined her bed. Then, "Mommy!"

Mrs. Rosso came running. "Jan?" she called.

"Mommy, look at my bed."

Mrs. Rosso took one look at the bed, then peered over at Hannah. "I wonder who could have short-sheeted Jan's bed," she said.

"Gosh, Mom. I don't know. Probably Woody," said Hannah.

Mrs. Rosso called Woody into the girls' room. Of course, he said that he had not touched Jan's bed. The other Rossos said the same thing. Hannah would not confess to her crime, though, so Mrs. Rosso simply helped Jan make up her bed again.

Nobody said another word about what had happened.

Two nights later, a shriek rang through the beach house.

It was a Saturday, and Mr. Rosso was there.

"Good grief!" he exclaimed. "Who was that?"

A few seconds later, Abbie came sheepishly into the living room where Mr. and Mrs. Rosso were reading, and Hannah, Woody, Hardy, and Candy were trying to watch television. (The reception on Fire Island was very poor. All grainy and wavy.)

"Sorry, everybody," said Abbie. "That was me. I just found *this*" (she held something gingerly between her thumb and forefinger) "under my pillow. It's a spider—a real one—but at least it's dead."

"Now how did that get there?" asked Mr. Rosso suspiciously. Both he and Mrs. Rosso eyed Hannah, but Hannah didn't move. She gazed at the TV set.

"Hannah?" said Mr. Rosso. "*Hannah?*"

"Okay, okay, I did it," Hannah confessed. "Sheesh."

The Rossos docked Hannah one week's allowance, but Hannah didn't care. In fact, two days later, Hannah got a brilliant idea. She was tired of the little practical jokes she'd been pulling off. They were too easy. She needed a bigger challenge. Her idea came when she was wandering down the beach one day and caught sight of Abbie with her new friends, Mel, Lacey, and Justin. If she could get Justin alone for a moment . . .

Surprisingly, Hannah *did* find Justin alone. It was the next morning, and she was walking Keegan in his stroller. She had decided to take him to the Harbor

Store and buy a Popsicle for herself. And who should she run into as she poked through the freezer, but Justin Hart himself.

"Hi!" said Hannah brightly. "I'm Hannah Rosso, Abbie's sister." She paused, pretending to look embarrassed. "Um, hey, isn't it funny that we should bump into each other?"

Justin flashed his movie-star smile at her. "Why is it funny?" he asked.

"Because Abbie wanted me to tell you something. She's too shy to tell you herself, so I said I would do it. Only I didn't know where to find you. And I wouldn't want to bother you when you're working on your movie."

"What's Abbie's message?" asked Justin, still smiling.

Hannah whispered something in Justin's ear. Then she fled from the store with Keegan, not bothering to buy a Popsicle after all.

She waited for results.

She got them the next day. Abbie left the house early in the morning to join Mel and Lacey who were going to watch Justin shoot a very sentimental scene on the beach that day. But she returned a half an hour later.

She was crying.

"Abbie, what's wrong?" asked Mrs. Rosso, genuinely concerned, since Abbie rarely cried.

"Mel and Lacey are mad at me," she said. "Justin told them that I said I have a crush on him. I never said that! I mean, I think he's cute and nice and everything, but he's Mel's boyfriend. I would never try to break them up. And that's what Mel accused me of."

"Oh, sweetie," said Mrs. Rosso. She sat on the couch, pulling Abbie down next to her. She put her arms around her. "Did you tell the kids you didn't do anything wrong?"

Abbie shook her head. "I guess I should have, but I was too surprised. And now Mel's so mad she's giving me the silent treatment."

The silent treatment lasted until the weekend. On Saturday, Abbie woke up and announced, "Today I'm going to talk to Melanie. I'm going to tell her I don't know what Justin was talking about. She can believe me or not. It's up to her."

Melanie must have believed Abbie. She and Lacey forgave her. They were friends again. Hannah grew bored. She would have to think of something else to do. She decided to concentrate on Candy. She already knew Candy was an easy target.

Hannah was jealous of Candy. Candy had gotten a room to herself that summer. Hannah had never had a room to herself. To make things worse, she had to share with Jan, who was the biggest baby in the world. Jan was a tattle-tale, and Ira lavished attention on her, and *some*times Mrs. Rosso gave her special privileges even though Keegan was the true baby of the family. If only Hannah had discovered the little bedroom in time, maybe it could have been hers. But Candy had found it first and had claimed it.

One night, Hannah waited until she was sure everyone in her family was asleep. She crept out the back door and walked along the deck to the window of Candy's room. She made sure the window was open. Then she moaned, "IIIII ammmmm the ghooooost next dooooor. . . . IIIII ammmmm the ghooooost of the seeeea!" She made her voice rise to a squeak. "You dooooon't haaaaave much tiiiiime leeeeeft."

When she heard Candy gasp, Hannah darted back into the house and jumped in bed. Candy didn't say anything the next morning about hearing ghosts, but from the look in her eyes, Hannah knew she had heard all right. Just like she had heard Hannah moaning, weeks ago.

The following night, Hannah waited again until everyone was asleep. This time she tiptoed into Candy's room and left two seashells on the windowsill. In the morning she was awakened by a shriek.

It was Candy. "Aughh!" she cried. "The ghost of the sea has been here!"

Hannah had to put her hand over her mouth to keep from laughing.

"What?" Mrs. Rosso rushed into Candy's room. Hannah followed her.

"The ghost of the sea," said Candy breathlessly. She was standing by the window, still wearing her nightgown. "Two nights ago he was calling for me. And last night he left *these*" (Candy gingerly held out the seashells) "on the windowsill. They're a sign. He really is coming to get me."

"Oh, Candy," said practical Mrs. Rosso, "you must have been *dreaming* about ghosts. And you probably left the shells on the sill yourself. You kids have been collecting shells ever since we got here."

"I—I didn't do those things," said Candy. But Mrs. Rosso was not convinced.

Hannah smiled to herself. This was fun! The summer was becoming much more interesting. She planned her next trick. It was going to be simple. After that, she would try something more difficult.

Hannah knew that Candy would be careful not to leave anything on her windowsill again. Not after Mrs. Rosso had hinted that Candy was just absentminded. So that night, Hannah once again tiptoed into her sister's room. This time, she left a crab claw on the sill.

The result was amazing. Candy awakened the entire family at six o'clock the next morning when she got up to use the bathroom and saw the claw.

"He's back! He's back! He's back!" she shrieked. "The ghost of the sea has been here again!" Candy was practically hysterical, and only Bainbridge was able to go to sleep again that morning. Everyone else was up for the day. (Well, Keegan was up until his first nap of the day.)

Wow, thought Hannah. She set about planning her next trick. It involved three seashells, a note, and a squirt gun. Hannah had to buy a squirt gun at the Harbor Store. She'd thought Woody had brought one to Fire Island, but she couldn't find it anywhere. Oh well. The squirt gun only cost $2.98. That wasn't much money, considering what Hannah had saved from her allowance, and it was good to have a squirt gun around. You never knew when you might need one. Then she quickly collected the shells, and after that she wrote the note.

Hannah waited until midnight to set things in motion. When she looked at her watch in the moonlight and saw both hands pointing to twelve, she crept into Candy's room and left the shells and the note on the windowsill. The note said, in wobbly, ghostlike writing: Watch out. I'm still coming for you, Candy. —The Ghost of the Sea.

Then Hannah tiptoed to Candy's doorway. "Caaaaan-deeeee . . . Caaaaan-deeeee . . ." she whispered.

"Mmphh?" said Candy, coming to.

That was when Hannah squirted her in the face twice with her new water pistol and then fled back to her room.

Of course, Candy awakened the entire household *again*, screaming about the ghost of the sea.

"He was here!" she cried to her mother. "I'm all wet. And a sea ghost would be wet, wouldn't he?"

"I don't know," said Mrs. Rosso with a sigh. And then, as everyone looked on, Hannah's mother spotted the note on the windowsill. She read it aloud. She looked at it for a long time. Finally she said, "Hannah, come to my room, please."

Reluctantly, Hannah followed her mother. Mrs. Rosso closed the door to the bedroom behind them and pointed to a chair. Hannah sat in it.

"This note is in your handwriting, Hannah," said her mother.

Hannah nodded her head. She'd been caught.

"You're grounded for a day," pronounced Mrs. Rosso. "You'll spend tomorrow inside. And before you go back to bed, I want you to apologize to your sister."

"Okay."

Hannah apologized to Candy. She spent the next day indoors, bored out of her skull. Mrs. Rosso wouldn't even let her watch TV.

For several days, nothing happened to Candy. Then on a Saturday night, with Mr. Rosso on the island for the weekend, the entire Rosso family went out to dinner at Davis Park's only restaurant. (The waiters had to move three tables together to make room for them.) When they returned to the beach house, Hannah was surprised to hear screams coming (once again) from Candy's room.

"He's back!" cried Candy. "My room is all wet!"

"I didn't do it," said Hannah immediately. "I was at the restaurant with everyone else."

"That lets me off the hook, too," said Woody.

"Then there really is a ghost!" said Candy hysterically.

Mr. Rosso sighed. Mrs. Rosso told him what had been going on. "I'm sure there's a logical explanation for this," he said, looking at the puddle on Candy's floor. Then he glanced up. "And there it is," he said. "The roof leaks, Candy. This is water from the rain we had during dinner. Bainbridge and I will patch up the roof tomorrow."

"How come the roof never leaked before?" asked Candy.

"Because the hole probably wasn't big enough," said Mr. Rosso.

The next day, Bainbridge and Mr. Rosso fixed the roof of the beach house. And the day after that, when Hannah was taking Keegan for a morning stroll, she met a girl her own age who was also pushing a baby in a stroller.

The girl smiled at Hannah. "Who's that?" she asked, pointing at Keegan.

"My little brother," replied Hannah.

"Oh. This is my brother, too. I'm Jennifer. His name is Jacob."

"I'm Hannah, and this is Keegan."

"Want to walk together?" asked Jennifer.

"Sure," replied Hannah.

She had a friend at last.

5

Ira and the Hospital Adventure

The signs were everywhere.

"Caution," they read. "Deer Ticks May Carry Lyme Disease."

The signs terrified Ira. They were the one thing about Fire Island that he truly did not like. Okay, the sand that got in the house, on the kitchen counters, somehow even in his bed—that was not great. And the mosquitoes and gnats and beach flies bothered him. Ira liked things neat and tidy. And he was afraid of germs. But the idea of Lyme disease bothered him much more than sand or insects.

When Ira first saw the signs about Lyme disease, he said to himself, All I have to do is stay away from deer.

Then one day someone went around sticking pamphlets about Lyme disease under everyone's front door. Ira saw the pamphlet first. He read it carefully. It listed the symptoms of Lyme disease and told about the ticks that carry it. The ticks, the leaflet said, could fall onto you from a tree branch. They could get caught on your clothes as you passed by a bush. They were all over the island.

All right, thought Ira, then I will just check myself for ticks a couple of times each day. Ira had seen ticks before. He knew what they looked like. And they were easy to spot.

But then Ira read the rest of the pamphlet and found out that deer ticks are different. They're no bigger than the period at the end of a sentence.

Oh no! thought Ira. I could check myself all over and miss something that tiny. What if one got in my *hair*? Then I'd never find it. Ira wondered if his mother would let him shave his head. He decided she wouldn't.

"This is terrible," Ira said aloud. He was alone in the beach house. He had come in for a drink of water and found no one at home. His brothers and sisters were scattered, and his mother had gone to the Harbor Store.

It was just Ira and the pamphlet—the truth about Lyme disease.

Ira read the pamphlet two or three times. The only good thing about Lyme disease, he decided, was that it couldn't kill you. It could, however, make you pretty sick. It could even *paralyze* you for a while. Ira did not want that.

It's not fair, thought Ira. I can keep my room neat (or at least my half of my room). I can brush the sand out of my bed every morning. I can pick up trash to keep our beach clean. I can keep my clothes neat. But how can I watch out for deer ticks?

"You can't," said Mrs. Rosso when Ira finally told her what was bothering him. "You can be careful, but you might not be able to prevent a deer tick from finding its way to your body."

"Ohh," moaned Ira.

"Listen, honey," began Mrs. Rosso. "We *do* need to be careful. We really do. But look out there." She pointed to the beach. "Look at those people. *They* don't have Lyme disease. If *every*body got Lyme disease, no one would come to Fire Island. So be careful, but stop worrying so much."

And Ira *did* stop worrying. When he and his family had been on the island for several weeks and everyone had stayed healthy, Ira began to forget about the deer ticks. There was so much to *do* on the island. He and Jan built endless castles in the sand and learned all sorts of tricks, like how to build moats and tunnels to let the water drain out of their castles. Sometimes they walked along the beach to where Abbie's friend Justin was working on his movie. He and Jan were even allowed to go to the Harbor Store by themselves and get ice-cream cones or Popsicles. There was, in fact, so much to do that Ira began to feel tired all the time. "It's all the sun," he said to Jan, when he had to take a break from the truly fantastic castle they were building.

"Then *that* ought to make you happy," said Jan, pointing to the sky.

Ira looked up. Thunderclouds were building on the horizon. "Ooh," he said. "We're going to have a storm tonight. A big one." Then he added quickly, "It'll be all right, Jan. Daddy's here." (It was a Saturday.) "He'll tell stories, and you'll forget about the storm."

Ira didn't mind thunderstorms, but Jan hated them. The storm hit early that evening and was tremendous. The sky darkened quickly, and right after that, torrents of rain began to fall. Thunder crashed, and with the first flash of lightning, the electricity went off.

Ira looked out the window and down the walk. "The electricity's off everywhere. I don't see a single light."

"Oh, nooo," moaned Jan.

But as soon as supper was over, Mr. Rosso said, "Who would like to hear a Mister Piebald story? I've thought of a new one."

"Me!" cried Jan, Ira, Hannah, and the twins. (The others had decided they were too old to hear Mr. Piebald stories.)

"Well," began Mr. Rosso when the five children were cuddled up with him on the couch, "there was once a tiny little man—"

"Mr. Piebald!" said Jan.

"That's right," agreed Mr. Rosso. "And he lived in a tree that was an apartment building. He lived on one floor, and Mr. and Mrs. Squirrel lived on the floor below."

Ira tried to listen to the story, but he was getting an awful headache. In fact, he felt sort of achey all over. Finally, he had to interrupt his father and say, "Daddy, I'm really tired. I think I'll go to bed."

Ira went to his room. He undressed very carefully, folding his clothes and putting them in the drawers or the hamper or hanging them in the closet. Ira was just about to pull on his pajamas when he noticed something. On his leg, he saw two round red welts, each surrounding a tiny black dot.

"Mommy!" Ira shrieked. "Daddy!"

In a second, Mr. and Mrs. Rosso had rushed into Ira's room. The other kids crowded in the doorway. "What's wrong, honey?" asked Mrs. Rosso.

"Look!" said Ira, holding out his leg. He felt panicky. "I don't feel good. Like I have the flu or something. And now I just found these bites. See the little black things in the middle of them? I think they're those tiny, tiny deer ticks."

Mr. Rosso examined Ira's bites. "You might be right," he said.

Mr. and Mrs. Rosso quickly bundled Ira into the wagon on the deck. They left Bainbridge and Abbie in charge of the other kids and hurried through the dark along the rain-soaked boardwalks to Bedside Manor, the house and office of the Davis Park doctor. Mrs. Rosso knocked on the door loudly.

"Hello?" she called. "Hello?"

A young woman came to the door. She was carrying a candle. "Yes?" she said.

"We're looking for the doctor," Mr. Rosso said. "We think our son has Lyme disease. He's not feeling too well."

"Well, I'm the doctor," said the woman. "I'm Doctor Yanoff. Come on around to the infirmary, and we'll check things out. We'll have to work by flashlight."

Mr. and Mrs. Rosso pulled Ira to a side door of Bedside Manor. Inside was a room that looked just like a doctor's office. The Rossos introduced themselves to Dr. Yanoff. Then they showed her the bites on Ira's leg.

"I just found them tonight," said Ira.

"How have you been feeling lately?" asked Dr. Yanoff.

"Sort of tired. And I ache. Like when I had the flu last winter."

"Well, that certainly sounds like Lyme disease," said Dr. Yanoff. "I've seen a few cases of it this week. But in order to be sure, I'll have to take a little blood from your finger. Do you mind needle sticks?"

"Yes," said Ira, but he had to have one anyway. "*Ow!*" he yelled.

"Sorry," the doctor told him. "Now, just to be on the safe side, I'm going to start you on penicillin. It won't hurt you if you don't have Lyme disease. And if you do have it, then we'll get a head start on treating you."

"Oh, wait!" exclaimed Mrs. Rosso. "Ira's allergic to penicillin."

"Hmm. In that case," replied Dr. Yanoff, "I'd like Ira to spend the night in the hospital on the mainland. The doctors there can try him on a different medication and observe him for a while. So why don't one of you go back to your house and get a few things for Ira while I call the hospital and also try to treat Ira's bites."

They all did as they were told. Ira lay on the table in the doctor's office feeling very sorry for himself. His head ached more and more, and he didn't have any energy. He wasn't sure he could even get off the table by himself. He let his mother stroke his forehead while he waited for his father to come back and for Dr. Yanoff to call the hospital and make arrangements.

When Mr. Rosso returned to Bedside Manor, he was carrying two small bags.

"What's in those?" asked Ira weakly.

"Well, one bag contains things for your mother. In the other are your pajamas, your slippers, and your toothbrush."

Ira nodded, and Dr. Yanoff hung up the telephone. "Okay," she said, "If you hurry, you can catch the last ferry from the island tonight. I'll arrange to have a cab meet you at the boat dock and drive you to the hospital. A Doctor Wertheimer will meet you in the emergency room and then take you to a bed in pediatrics."

"Let's get going, then," said Mr. Rosso.

"Mommy?" said Ira. "I don't think I can get up."

"Poor baby," replied Mrs. Rosso. She and Ira's father lifted him gently from the table and carried him out to the wagon.

"Storm's letting up," said Dr. Yanoff. "That's good. It means the ferry crossing won't be too rough. Good luck, Ira!"

The Rossos thanked Dr. Yanoff. Then they hurried along the boardwalks under dripping trees and a black, black sky.

"Are you coming to the hospital, Daddy?" asked Ira from his bed in the wagon.

"Nope," he replied. "I'd like to, but I better stay at home with that zoo we call our family. Your mom will stick with you all the way, though. Okay?"

"Okay," murmured Ira.

The Rossos reached the ferry dock as the last few passengers were boarding. Ordinarily, on a Saturday night, the last ferry from Davis Park would be crowded. Anyone who had come to Fire Island for dinner at the restaurant or to visit friends had to leave then or spend the night on the island. But the stormy weather had kept people at home. So Ira and his mother were two of just six passengers on the boat that night.

Mrs. Rosso held Ira in her lap, their bags next to

them. They waved good-bye to Mr. Rosso on the dock, although he was hard to see through the foggy windows. The ferry had barely left the dock and was chugging loudly across the sound, when Ira fell asleep.

He did not wake up until he heard his mother say softly, "Ira. Honey. Ira? We're here. Come on. You've got to wake up."

"Okay." Ira tried to raise his head, but it hurt terribly. He felt so weak that he couldn't stand up. Finally, his mother had to take the bags off the ferry and then come back for Ira. Even though Ira was nine years old, he allowed his mother to pick him up and carry him to the waiting taxi.

In the taxi, he dozed. He dozed until once again he heard Mrs. Rosso say, "Ira. Honey? We're at the hospital."

The hospital.

Oh boy. Ira did *not* want to be there. Hospitals meant needles and medicine and doctors poking you, and most of all—sick people. I could come home from the hospital sicker than I already am, thought Ira. Germs, germs everywhere.

But Ira had no choice. Before he knew it, he'd met Dr. Wertheimer, been through the emergency room, and was riding in a wheelchair to a room in the children's wing.

Ira's room had only two beds, and both were empty. Good, thought Ira. Fewer germs.

Mrs. Rosso helped Ira into his pajamas, and then he climbed wearily into bed. But before he could fall asleep, Dr. Wertheimer was back. She examined Ira again. She talked to his mother. And then she gave Ira some pills to swallow. "Yuck," said Ira. He was afraid the pills would get caught in his throat, but they didn't.

"Mommy?" said Ira, looking around the room. "Are you going to stay with me?"

"Yup," replied his mother. "The hospital is bending the rules a little. The nurses are letting me sleep in the other bed. We'll probably only be here overnight."

Ira wasn't sleepy anymore. He'd gotten a lot of sleep on the ferry and in the cab. Also, he felt a little better. Was the medicine working already?

"You know," said Ira, sitting up. "This is one of the most interesting things that has ever happened to me."

Mrs. Rosso smiled. She had changed into a nightgown and robe in the bathroom. Now she was sitting on the edge of her bed. "It's certainly been an adventure," she agreed.

"First the storm and the blackout," said Ira, "and now the hospital. I'm sure glad the hospital has electricity. I wouldn't want to be here in the dark."

"I think the power failure is over," Mrs. Rosso told him.

"Mommy?" said Ira, who had just thought of a question about blackouts.

"Honey, I thought you were sleepy. I thought you wanted to go to bed."

"I did," said Ira. "But now I'm feeling better."

Mrs. Rosso was about to tell Ira to save his conversation for the morning when a nurse came into the room, smiled, and said cheerfully, "Lights out. Bedtime." Then he flicked off the lamps and left.

"Lights out?" whispered Ira.

"Hospital rules, I guess," replied Mrs. Rosso. "Good night, sleep tight, don't let the bedbugs bite."

"Or the deer ticks," added Ira.

When Ira awoke the next morning, the first thing he noticed was that his mother's bed was empty—and all made up.

"Mommy?" called Ira. And then, feeling nervous, *"Mommy?"*

A different nurse came into the room, a tall nurse with dark skin and dark hair. "Well," she said, "I was wondering when you'd wake up. Don't worry about your mom. She's gone to the gift shop. She'll be right back. You can eat breakfast while you wait for her."

Ira could hear a cart rattling down the hall. "What's for breakfast?" he asked. He thought he could smell toast.

"Toast and cream-of-wheat cereal," answered the nurse. "And a banana."

"Oh," said Ira. He hated cream-of-wheat cereal. He wished his mother would come back soon.

She did. She arrived in time to catch the horrified look on Ira's face when the orderly uncovered the breakfast tray and Ira saw the cereal. As soon as the orderly was gone, Mrs. Rosso said, "Don't worry, Ira. Look what I got you for breakfast." She opened a small paper bag and pulled out two chocolate-covered granola bars and a little container of ice cream.

"Ice cream! Ice cream for breakfast!" cried Ira.

"*Shh!*" hissed Mrs. Rosso. "Yes. Just this once. But I'm sure the hospital wouldn't approve, so eat it quietly, and I'll eat your breakfast."

Ira ate. He felt hungry. He realized he hadn't felt quite so hungry in a long time. While he was eating (and he ate the granola bars first, saving the ice cream for last), he noticed another bag sitting at the end of his mother's bed.

"What's that?" he asked. The bag looked like the one the ice cream and granola bars had come in, but it was bigger.

"You'll see," replied Mrs. Rosso. "I'll let you open it after you've eaten—and after you've taken your pills."

"More pills?" said Ira, dismayed.

"I'm afraid so. You're going to be taking them for about a month."

"A *month*?"

"Yes. They're already helping you. You look much better than you did last night."

"Okay," replied Ira. He could deal with that. He didn't want Lyme disease to paralyze him, especially not at the beach.

So Ira finished his breakfast and took his pills. Then he eyed the bag at the end of Mrs. Rosso's bed. She handed it to him. Ira peeked inside. He saw two speed-cars and a transformer that changed from a motorcycle into a dinosaur. "Cool!" cried Ira. "Thanks, Mommy."

At eleven o'clock, the phone rang in Ira's room. "Can I get it?" he asked.

"Of course," said Mrs. Rosso.

Ira picked up the receiver. "Hello?" he said.

At the other end of the line he heard a chorus of voices singing, to the tune of *Happy Birthday*, "Get we-ell to you! Get we-ell to you! Get we-ell, dear Ira. Get we-ell to you!"

Ira grinned. It was the rest of his family. (Well, except for Keegan.) "Hi!" he said. "I have Lyme dis-ease, but I'm feeling much better. I got ice cream for breakfast. But I have to take pills for a whole month."

"Ice cream for breakfast?" repeated Jan. "Lucky duck."

"And—and, hey! There's a clown in the hall!" exclaimed Ira. "Honest. He has a big red nose and green frizzy hair, and . . . he's coming into my room. I have to go now. 'Bye!"

Ira hung up the phone excitedly. He had never been so close to a clown before.

The clown clomped over to Ira's bed in his long, floppy clown shoes. Then he honked a horn that he was hiding behind his back. He didn't say a word, but he grinned at Ira, blew up some skinny balloons, and twisted them into the shape of a giraffe. He handed the giraffe to Ira, honked his horn once more, and flumped out of the room, tripping over his feet in the doorway.

Ira began to laugh and couldn't stop. "That was funny!" he finally gasped.

Mrs. Rosso was laughing, too. Then she said, "Guess what. Good news. I spoke to Doctor Wertheimer, and you can go home this afternoon."

"Really?" said Ira. "Gosh. The hospital is sort of fun."

Fun or not, Ira was discharged from the hospital at two o'clock that afternoon. An orderly brought a wheelchair to Ira's room and helped him into it.

"But I can walk," protested Ira.

"Sorry," said the orderly with a smile. "Hospital rules." He rushed Ira down the hallway, shouting, "Vroom! Vroom!"

"Wait for me!" called Mrs. Rosso.

Outside the entrance to the hospital, a cab was waiting. Mrs. Rosso climbed in first, carrying the overnight bags, the toys, and the balloon giraffe. The orderly lifted Ira into the cab, and the trip back to Fire Island began. First, the ride to the ferry, then the ferry to Davis Park.

When the ferry had reached the dock, turned around so that it was facing Patchogue again, and the motor had finally ground to a halt, Ira and his mother joined the line of passengers and made their way to the exit.

Ira was stepping off the ramp when a crowd of people began jumping up and down, shouting, "Ira! Ira! Welcome home!"

Ira blinked in the sunlight. It was his family. Faustine and Dinnie were holding up a banner they had made that read: "Welcome Home, Ira!" Hardy was pulling the Sandpiper House wagon. It was decorated with crêpe paper and balloons and was lined with pillows.

"That's your chariot," said Jan grandly.

Ira climbed in. He could not remember when he had had so much attention. His father kissed him, Abbie hugged him, Hannah handed him a seashell, and Keegan blew him a raspberry.

"Thanks!" was all Ira could say.

Hardy pulled Ira along in the wagon. People on the dock stared and smiled.

Ira waved to a couple of them. He felt like a celebrity.

Back at Sandpiper House, Mrs. Rosso fixed a place on the couch in the living room near the window. Ira was surrounded by his toys, and everyone kept bringing him juice. And he could look out the window at the people on the beach. Jan went outside and built a huge sand castle for him.

*   *   *

After dinner that evening, Abbie's friends Melanie and Justin dropped by.

"How's the patient?" Mel asked Ira.

"Much better, thank you," said Ira politely. He felt like a king. Mel had brought Ira a little puzzle, and Justin had brought him a kite.

"As soon as you're well enough, we'll fly it together," Justin told Ira. Then he turned to Abbie. "I have an announcement to make," he said. "Do you think you could get your brothers and sisters in here?"

"Sure," replied Abbie. "Hey, everybody!" she yelled. "Come here!"

Bainbridge, Candy, Woody, Hardy, Faustine, Dinnie, Hannah, and Jan ran into the living room. "Do you need Keegan?" teased Abbie.

"No," said Justin, grinning.

"What's going on?" asked Hardy.

"I have some news," answered Justin. "Today the director announced that pretty soon we're going to need lots of extras for the movie."

"Extra what?" asked Jan.

"Extra people."

"Like for crowd scenes?" asked Abbie.

"Exactly," said Justin. (Abbie looked quite pleased with herself.) "So," Justin went on, "I am personally inviting all of you—even Keegan because we need babies—to be in the movie. What you have to do is—"

But Justin was interrupted by Dinnie. "We're going to be in a movie?" she shrieked. "In a *movie*? Oh, my gosh, I can't believe it!"

"Everyone will see us!" cried Hardy. "Cool!"

"I'll be up on the big screen with you and all those stars," said Candy, dreamily.

"Plus you get paid," added Justin. "Fifty dollars for each day you work."

"*Fifty dollars!*" (That was Faustine.) "Maybe we could pay the fishermen to stop killing fish!"

"Are you crazy?" exclaimed Hannah. "With fifty dollars—or more—we could buy half the toys in the world."

"I'll be a millionaire!" cried Woody.

"Oh boy," said Ira. "I hope I get well soon. I want to be in the movie, too."

"Well, I'll let you guys know when we need you. But I'm warning you. It's hard work. You have to do things over and over. The day can be long."

Ira didn't care. Nobody cared. They were going to be in a *movie*.

Ira decided that the last two days had been the best in his life.

6

Janthina and the Beauty Treatment

"Keegan, Keegan. Baby Beegan," said Jan in a sing-song voice.

She looked at her little brother, who was sitting in his stroller. He was gumming up a teething biscuit. Abbie was cooing to him, "Hi, Keegie. Hi, Keegie," and Keegan was smiling. Or sometimes he would laugh and spray the teething biscuit everywhere.

It was like this almost every morning. The Rossos got up. They ate breakfast. Some of the kids would go outside to the beach. And the rest would stay inside for a while, making a fuss over Keegan.

"At least *you* still like me," said Jan to Zsa-Zsa. She put out her hand to pat the cat—and Zsa-Zsa jumped into Keegan's lap, which made Keegan laugh again. This time he sprayed the teething biscuit at Jan.

"Gross! Cut it out!" cried Jan.

"Janthina, don't yell at the baby," said Mrs. Rosso.

I used to be the baby until *he* came along, thought Jan.

"Keegan, Keegan. Baby Beegan," she muttered again.

Abbie turned around and gave Jan a *look*. It wasn't fair, Jan thought. At first Keegan had just been a cute little baby. Everyone peeked in his crib or wanted to give him bottles. But there wasn't much else you could do with a baby as young as Keegan.

Then Keegan got bigger. And bigger. He learned how to smile and then how to laugh. Now everyone spent time sitting with Keegan, trying to make him laugh.

When *I* was the youngest, my brothers and sisters paid lots of attention to *me*, thought Jan. Abbie took care of me, Bainbridge made toys for me, and Mommy and Daddy bought me almost anything I wanted. Now it's Keegan, Keegan, Keegan. Even Ira doesn't play with me so much, but that's because he got Lyme disease. Jan hoped Ira would hurry up and get better.

One Friday, Mr. Rosso arrived on Fire Island with news. "Guess what. We're going to have guests next week when I'm on vacation."

"Who?" asked Mrs. Rosso. She looked alarmed. She was probably already planning systems for beds and bedding and meals and how to keep extra sand out of the house.

"Nanny and Grandy," replied Mr. Rosso.

"Goody!" cried Jan. Nanny and Grandy always paid lots of attention to her. And they usually brought gifts.

"Anyone else?" asked Mrs. Rosso.

Jan didn't hear the answer. She had quit paying attention. She was hoping that Nanny and Grandy would bring her the Puffin' Pal doll she wanted so badly. She *knew* her grandparents knew she wanted the doll because she had written them a postcard that had said:

Dear Nanny and Grandy,
      I love Fire Island. The beach is fun. How are you? I am fine. I really, really, really, really, really want a Puffin' Pal doll. A pink one.
                              Love, Jan xxoo

The next week, Mr. Rosso reached the island earlier than usual. Jan knew he was going to arrive on an early ferry, so she and the twins ran to meet the boat.

Jan couldn't wait to see her pink Puffin' Pal doll. But she didn't get to see it at all.

"Look!" cried Dinnie. She was pointing to the top of the ferry where Mr. Rosso was waving. Next to him were Nanny and Grandy (they were waving, too), and next to *them* were Uncle Jimmy, Aunt Martha, and Scott, Lyman, Courtenay, and Eleanor.

"Who said *they* could come?" asked Jan, staring with dismay at her cousins.

"Dad said last week that they were coming," replied Faustine, sounding surprised. "He said Nanny and Grandy, Uncle Jimmy, Aunt Martha, Courtenay, Eleanor, Lyman, and Scott. Didn't you hear?"

"No," said Jan. She'd been too busy thinking about a Puffin' Pal doll.

"Well, aren't you glad to see them?" asked Dinnie. "We haven't seen our cousins in ages. Uncle Jimmy or Aunt Martha, either. I can't wait to play with Courtenay and Scott on the beach."

"Courtenay and Scott are your age," muttered Jan.

The *Kiki* sputtered to a halt, after turning around to face Patchogue again.

The people on the top of the ferry began to climb down the stairs. Soon Jan's father, grandparents, aunt, uncle, and cousins were rushing down the gangplank, and everyone began hugging.

"What a wonderful reception!" exclaimed Nanny.

Jan looked for bags that might hold gifts—like a Puffin' Pal doll—but she didn't see any. Only suitcases and hats and sandbuckets. The sandbuckets were for Eleanor and Lyman. They were four and two, lots littler than Jan. Now everyone would fuss over Eleanor and Lyman as well as Keegan.

Jan was just a plain old kid in the middle. She was not special anymore.

At Sandpiper House that night, Mrs. Rosso organized and organized. She had already decided how the bedrooms would be divided up. Nanny and Grandy got their own room, and so did Uncle Jimmy and Aunt Martha. Bainbridge and Woody had to sleep on the couches in the living room, and the rest of the kids slept three or four in a room, except for Candy.

Jan and Hannah wound up with Lyman and Eleanor.

After dinner, while it was still light outside, the Rossos and their guests sat on the big deck overlooking the ocean.

Lyman waved to the waves, and everyone laughed. Nanny said, "Isn't he adorable? Waving to the waves?"

Grandy held Keegan on his lap and played pat-a-cake with him. When Keegan laughed, so did everyone else. (But not Jan.)

Eleanor said she could turn a cartwheel. When she tried, her parents, Mr. and Mrs. Rosso, and Nanny and Grandy clapped, even though Eleanor had not turned a real cartwheel at all.

"*I* can turn a cartwheel," said Jan. Jan took gymnastics during the school year, so she turned a perfect cartwheel.

Eleanor cried. Her parents comforted her.

The adults—plus Bainbridge and Abbie—even made a fuss over Zsa-Zsa. "She's precious," said Aunt Martha.

Jan wished she could say that she had found and rescued Zsa-Zsa when Zsa-Zsa was a kitten. But she hadn't. The twins had. So she kept her mouth closed.

That night was one of the longest of Jan's life. It seemed even longer than Christmas Eve, when Jan would wait and wait and wait for morning to come. Eleanor had to go to the bathroom three times, and each time she woke up Jan because she was scared to go by herself, and Hannah wouldn't wake up. Lyman mumbled in his sleep and then had a nightmare, so Jan had to comfort him and remind him where he was and tell him everything was okay.

The next morning, Jan told her mother about her awful night.

"Eleanor and Lyman are scared of everything. Eleanor wouldn't go to the bathroom by herself, and Lyman had a bad dream. I had to talk and talk to him before he went back to sleep."

"Jan," said Mrs. Rosso, looking surprised. "I'm very proud of you. You had a tough night, but you did all the right things."

"I did?" said Jan. She smiled. Then she thought, Today I will be very helpful.

Jan folded laundry for her mother. She helped make

lunch. She walked Eleanor to the Harbor Store and bought her a Popsicle. But by dinnertime, nobody was saying how wonderful and helpful Jan was.

On Sunday, Jan's cousins were playing on the deck. Their mother was watching them. Mrs. Rosso was holding Keegan and watching them, too.

"Lyman is so advanced," said Mrs. Rosso to Aunt Martha. "Look at how he's stacking those blocks, and he's only two."

Aunt Martha smiled.

"And look at Courtenay," Mrs. Rosso went on. "She reads to herself now."

"Look what I can do," spoke up Jan. She scrambled onto the deck railing, spread out her arms, and began to walk along it as if she were on a tightrope. She looked down and almost lost her balance, but she kept going.

"Jan!" screeched Mrs. Rosso. She jumped up, tossed Keegan into Uncle Jimmy's arms, grabbed Jan, and pulled her onto the deck.

"Don't you *ever* do that again!" she scolded. "It must be ten feet from the railing to the sand. You could have hurt yourself badly."

"Falling into sand?"

"There might be barbed wire or broken glass down there," replied Mrs. Rosso, still sounding angry. "Not to mention poison ivy."

Jan ran to her room and didn't come out until dinnertime. (But she let Ira come in and talk to her.)

Nobody paid attention to Jan. They didn't pay attention when she moped around the house all the next day, nor when she dressed up in her church clothes. (Well, Uncle Jimmy *did* tell her she looked pretty. But her father told her to take off her church clothes because it was not Sunday.)

By Thursday, Jan was tired of everything and everybody. In the morning, she left the house by herself and walked to the area where another scene for *Summer Blues* was being shot. None of her brothers or sisters was there. They were so used to seeing Justin Hart now that they didn't watch the moviemaking very often. They hung around with their friends or played on the beach unless something *really* interesting was happening with the movie.

Jan watched the action for a while. She decided that making a movie must be very difficult. Justin Hart and his co-star, Chloe, were trying to shoot one little scene. The only thing they had to do was face each other, holding hands, while Justin said, "I think it's over for the summer. We shouldn't see each other anymore." Then Chloe was supposed to burst into tears. But each time they were in the middle of a scene that Jan thought was going well, the director would yell, "Cut!" and then say something like, "There's a glare on Justin's face," or "Justin, look right into Chloe's eyes when you say that," or "Chloe, your eyes should *already* be filling with tears."

Finally, after about fifteen takes, the director said the scene looked okay. Justin and Chloe sagged into chairs under an umbrella.

"Hi, Justin," said Jan shyly, approaching him.

"Jan!" exclaimed Justin. "Are you here all by yourself?"

Jan nodded. "I'm just watching."

"Great," said Justin. "Have you met Chloe?"

Jan shook her head.

"Hi, Jan," said Chloe.

Jan took a good look at Chloe. And suddenly she decided that Chloe was the most beautiful person she'd ever seen. She was wearing a lot of makeup, Jan could tell. And her hair had been curled. She looked gorgeous.

"Justin?" said Jan, feeling shyer than ever. "Do you think—I mean, I know that probably no one can do this. But do you think that someone could make me look like . . . like Chloe?" Jan's voice dropped to a whisper.

Justin and Chloe grinned.

"Sure," said Justin. "It's kind of quiet around here. Let me take you to the makeup artist. Her name is Laura."

"Really?" squeaked Jan. "Oh, thank you, Justin!"

Jan waved good-bye to Chloe, and Justin led her to a beach house that the movie company had rented for the summer.

"Laura?" called Justin as he pulled open the screen door.

"Justin? Is that you? You need a touch-up?" called a voice.

"Nope. I've got a friend here who would like a—I guess she'd like a beauty treatment, wouldn't you, Jan?"

"Yes!" said Jan, gazing around the house. It didn't look a thing like the inside of hers. It looked partly like an office and partly like a very messy beauty parlor. Laura was seated on a stool in front of a mirror in the beauty parlor part. All around the mirror were light-bulbs. And on a table under the mirror were jars and tubes and bottles and creams and brushes and powder puffs.

"Ooh," said Jan. "I want to look beautiful like Chloe."

"Laura?" said Justin questioningly.

"I've got time," Laura answered.

"Thanks," replied Justin. "You'd be doing a real favor for a friend."

Jan smiled. Justin thought of her as his friend!

A call came from outside then. "Justin! They want you back for the next scene. Right now."

"Okay!" yelled Justin. He turned to Laura. "She's all yours. Have fun, Jan. I'll see you later."

Jan was left with Laura and the makeup.

"So," said Laura. "How do you want to look?"

"Just like Chloe," Jan replied.

"Want me to do anything to your hair?"

Jan hesitated. She looked at Laura's hair. It was not hair that Jan would want. It was poofy, and it was two different colors: black and very, very yellow.

Laura must have noticed Jan looking at *her* hair, because she said, "We can do anything you want to *your* hair. Maybe it would look pretty if I just curled it a little."

"Okay!" Jan only had her hair curled on very special occasions.

"All right," said Laura. "Let's put some hot rollers in your hair, and then we'll begin your makeup."

"Hot rollers?" repeated Jan. "How hot?"

"Oh, don't worry. They won't burn you. I promise. They just work really fast. Here. Climb up on this stool."

Jan climbed onto the stool and found herself facing the mirror with the lights around it. I, thought Jan, am going to look so beautiful that my family will *have* to notice me. I'll be cuter than Lyman or Eleanor—or Keegan or Zsa-Zsa. It won't matter who can stack blocks or who can turn cartwheels or anything else. Everyone will look at me and say how beautiful I am.

Laura began winding Jan's hair onto the spiky rollers. She lifted one strand at a time and wrapped it around and around a curler. Then she fastened the hair in place with things that looked like big bobby pins. The rollers were hotter than Jan had thought they'd be, but she didn't say anything. She didn't want to hurt Laura's feelings.

"There we are," said Laura finally. "All finished. Now we'll begin your face. Would you like me to paint your nails, too?"

"Oh yes!" cried Jan. This was getting better and better.

"Well then, maybe we should do your nails next so they can dry while I put on your makeup. Here are the colors I have. You choose one."

Jan looked and looked. She'd never seen so many colors, not even in a beauty parlor. At last she chose bright red. She had seen her mother wear bright red polish sometimes. Red lipstick, too.

Laura painted Jan's nails. It took a long time. First she rubbed cream on Jan's hands, then she put on *two* coats of polish, and finally she put on something called top coat. "That will keep the polish from chipping too fast," Laura told Jan. "Now we better take the curlers out of your hair. They've been in a long time. You keep your hands still so you don't smudge the polish before it dries."

"Okay," said Jan. She looked in the mirror, watching Laura remove the curlers. Each time she did, a huge curl sprang to the top of Jan's head. She had not expected to see such tight curls.

"Oh . . ." she said in dismay.

"Don't worry. They'll loosen up," Laura assured her. "And while they do, I'll put on your makeup."

For the next half hour, Laura put creams and powders on Jan's face. She put mascara, eyeliner, and shadow on her eyes. She put blush on her cheeks. Finally, she said, "Okay. What color lipstick?"

"Red," replied Jan. "To match my nails."

Laura put the lipstick on, but she used a tiny brush to do it. Jan had never seen her mother apply lipstick with a brush.

"There. All done," said Laura.

Jan stared at herself in the mirror. She looked beautiful—and at least ten years old. But her hair was still too curly and springy.

As if Laura could read Jan's mind, she said, "Just leave your hair alone. It'll begin to fall naturally. Especially in this hot weather."

"Okay," replied Jan. And then she remembered to thank Laura. "I have never looked so beautiful," she told her.

Jan ran all the way to Sandpiper House. When she got there, she discovered that everyone else was gone. Jan looked out the window. There they were, further down the beach.

"Perfect," said Jan aloud.

She dashed into the bathroom and examined herself in the mirror. She really did look spectacular—except for her hair. Jan decided to brush it out. She brushed and brushed, and before she knew it, her curls were *gone*.

"Oh no!" cried Jan. "*Now* what am I going to do? She looked in the medicine cabinet and found a pair of scissors. Maybe I could cut my hair, she thought. She began to trim away. When she was done, she thought the left side looked shorter than the right side. So she trimmed the right side. Then it looked shorter than the left side. So she trimmed the left side. By the time she heard her family coming home for lunch, Jan's hair was cut almost up to the top of her ears. But her face and her nails still looked great. So Jan waltzed into the living room.

"Hello," she said casually.

There were her parents, Nanny and Grandy, Aunt Martha and Uncle Jim, Abbie, Bainbridge, and the smallest children. For a moment, everyone stared at Jan. Jan was afraid that someone might laugh at her, but no one did. Finally, Mrs. Rosso said, "Honey, how beautiful you look. Who—who helped you get made up?"

"Laura," Jan replied. "She's the makeup person for *Summer Blues*. Do I look older?" she asked hopefully.

"At least twelve," said Bainbridge. He started to laugh, but he stopped quickly when his father glared at him.

"Older and gorgeous," said Aunt Martha.

Suddenly everyone was exclaiming over Jan. She

was the center of attention, just like when she had been the baby of the family.

But after lunch, Mrs. Rosso pulled Jan aside and said, "Jan, you do look very pretty. But you are not old enough to wear makeup. And I don't think Laura should have cut your hair without checking with your father or me first. I think I should have a talk with her."

Jan let her mother leave Sandpiper House and walk partway to Laura's before she ran after her. "Mommy! Mommy!" she called. "Laura didn't cut my hair. I did that myself." As they walked home together, Jan told her mother about the curls and the scissors.

"It isn't easy giving yourself a haircut," said Jan.

"No. And I don't want you to do that again. Ever. Do you understand?" said Mrs. Rosso firmly. Then she sent Jan to her room for the afternoon.

Darn, thought Jan. Now nobody can see me.

That night, when dinner was over, Mr. Rosso took Jan by the hand and said, "Let's walk down the beach."

"Okay," said Jan. Her father must want to show her off, she thought.

But Mr. Rosso had other things on his mind. "Sweetie," he said to Jan, "I guess it's hard not being the baby of the family anymore, isn't it?"

Jan hesitated. Then, "Yes," she admitted.

"But do you know what? No matter where you are in this family, you're special. And you'll always be important. Abbie is special because she's very responsible. Ira is special because—"

"Because he's neat?" suggested Jan.

Mr. Rosso laughed. "Okay. Because he's neat. And you're special because you're Jan and you have interesting ideas and you are good with little kids. Your mother and I love you very much—with or without makeup. I hope you know that."

"I guess I do," said Jan, who stopped to give her father a hug.

But she was still not sorry about her beauty treatment. In fact, as she lay in bed that night, she thought, Maybe I'll get another beauty treatment before the summer is over.

Jan fell asleep smiling.

7

Dagwood and the Million-Dollar Idea

Woody liked money. That was how it all began.

And the Harbor Store, small as it was, carried plenty of things Woody wanted to buy: there were kites, Davis Park visors, hats and sunglasses and beach towels and toys. If Woody walked through the wildlife preserve to the snack bar and store in the next community, he found even more great stuff to buy.

But Woody's allowance didn't begin to cover the things he wanted.

"Mom?" he said to his mother one Saturday. "Can I have a raise in my allowance?" Then he remembered to add, "Please?"

"*May* I have a raise?" Mrs. Rosso corrected him.

"May I?"

"Why?"

"So I can buy cool stuff. I saw a foam hat shaped like a lobster. That would be neat. I would love to get that. But I don't have enough money."

"You think I should raise your allowance so you can look like a lobster?"

Woody knew where this conversation was going. "No," he said.

"How about *earning* some money?" suggested Mrs. Rosso.

That was just like a mother, thought Woody. He wanted to say, "Forget it. Just forget it." Instead he said, "All *right*," and left Sandpiper House.

Woody decided to take a walk. He made his way toward the beach where he found a bunch of his brothers and sisters.

"What're you doing?" Hardy asked Woody.

"Thinking."

"About what?"

"About how to earn money. I want that lobster hat we saw."

Hardy was squatting in the sand, examining an empty clam shell. Woody walked right by him.

"Hey!" said Hardy, standing up. "Where are you going? Can I come with you?"

Before Woody could say yes or no, Hardy was running after him. They walked along the beach together.

"You need to go into business," said Hardy.

"I know," replied Woody. "But what can I do?"

"How about a lemonade stand?" asked Hardy.

"Baby stuff," replied Woody.

And then he noticed a small crowd gathered further down the beach. What was going on?

"Come on!" cried Woody.

Woody and Hardy ran to the crowd and worked their way to the front.

"Maybe a shark washed up on the beach!" said Woody.

Hardy tried to peer around a heavyset man. "Nah," he said. "It's just a couple of little kids making crayon designs on shells. Let's go."

"Wait!" exclaimed Woody. "A lady just gave those kids fifty cents for one of the shells. And it's only a clamshell with a stupid pink design on the back. Anyone could make that."

The boys looked at each other. They grinned. Then they backed out of the crowd. "*I* could make that," Woody continued. "And I could do it a thousand times better. Those kids are only about seven years old."

"What would you put on your shells?" asked Hardy.

"Oh, beach scenes and stuff. Except I would use paint, not crayons, and I would decorate the *insides* of the shells."

"I thought you hated art. You got a C minus in it last year."

"I don't hate art. I just hate Mrs. Pill."

"Mrs. Hill," Hardy corrected his brother.

"Well, anyway, all I need to do is collect clamshells—they're everywhere—and buy some good paint. Maybe Dad can get me some in the city this week. Boy, I bet I could become a millionaire. I could buy every lobster hat in the Harbor Store."

Mr. Rosso agreed to give Woody an advance on his allowance, and that week he did buy paints for him. Meanwhile, Woody collected all of the clamshells he could find. And when Mr. Rosso returned to Fire Island the following weekend, Woody got right to work. He had been practicing drawing sunsets and boats and fish and other beach things. Now he tried painting them on the smooth insides of the shells.

Not bad, he thought, when he looked at his first few attempts.

"What do you think?" he asked his father. "Be honest," he added.

Mr. Rosso looked at the shells critically. At last he said, "I think they're very good. What will people use them for?"

"Oh, you know, candy dishes," replied Woody, pleased with his father's approval.

"Or they could just be objets d'art," said Abbie, who had wandered into the living room. (She pronounced the words "ob-jay dar.")

"'Scuse me?" said Woody.

"Objets d'art. You know, nice things to look at."

"You mean like *art*?" said Woody witheringly. "Why don't you talk like a regular person?"

"All right, you two. Calm down," said Mr. Rosso.

Woody shot Abbie a *look*. Then he took the shells into his room.

Three days later, Woody had painted approximately thirty shells. That afternoon, he spread them out on the floor in the living room. Then he laid them in rows. He examined them for a long time.

Woody decided they were quite good. He also decided he needed more variety in his artwork, maybe some animals made from shells and stones. If he bought pipe cleaners and glue, he could get right to work.

Woody's first animal was a frog with a small clam-shell for its head, a stone for its body, pebbles for its feet, and pipe cleaners for its legs. Woody painted it green. Then he painted a face on it.

"That's adorable!" cried Abbie when she saw it. "I'll buy that. How much is it? I'll put it on my dresser."

"It's—it's a dollar twenty-five," said Woody. The price sounded high, but he'd worked hard on the frog.

"Great," said Abbie, and forked over a dollar and a quarter.

Woody stayed home for a few more days and created all sorts of things, mostly animals. His collection of things to sell grew so big that he didn't know how he was going to carry it from house to house. (He planned to be a door-to-door salesman.)

"Set up a stand," said Hardy sensibly.

A stand. That was a great idea. Woody could carry a small table to a spot near the ferry dock. He could set out his shells and stones and animals for people to buy. And in a bag next to him, he could store the rest of his work. That way he could keep the table full, so the supply wouldn't look as if it was getting too low. (Although Abbie pointed out that if the supply *did* look low, then people would think Woody's work was selling really well, and they'd want to buy *more*.)

Woody set up his stand late one Friday morning when weekenders were beginning to arrive on the ferry. Nearly everyone who got off the boat had to go past the stand. And nearly everyone stopped to look at Woody's creations.

"Aren't they darling!" said a woman, pointing to a collection of stones with teddy bears painted on them.

And "How sweet!" exclaimed someone else, looking at a group of shell-and-pipe-cleaner poodles.

"Yeah, *sweet*," said a third voice. Woody glanced up. The voice had come from a boy about his age. Woody hadn't noticed him on the island before. The boy put one hand on his hip. "And that little froggie is simply the *cutest*."

Woody could feel his heart pounding. He also felt a fight coming on. But several people were clamoring to buy things, so Woody tried to ignore the boy. He concentrated on selling a candy dish and some shell poodles. He had to think hard when he needed to make change.

The crowd slipped away as people continued toward their houses. At last everyone who had gotten off the ferry was gone. A few kids drifted into the Harbor Store to buy candy, but that was it. Woody was about to pack up his objets d'art when he realized that another ferryload of people would be coming soon. He sat down behind the stand and waited . . . and waited.

He almost fell asleep.

But he opened his eyes when he heard a familiar voice say, "My, they *are* darling," and another voice say, "Absolutely adorable."

Woody found himself looking at the boy who had teased him earlier. He was back, with two younger boys about Ira's age.

Woody glared at the boys. He could feel his fists tightening. He took a step back, getting ready to—

"Hey, Woody!"

Woody turned around. Ira was trotting along the boardwalk.

"Woody!" Ira called again. "Mommy wants you to baby-sit Keegan."

"Yeah. *Mommy* wants you to *baby*-sit," mimicked one of the boys.

Woody unclenched his fists. He decided he'd better

not have a fight while Ira was looking on. So he packed up his shells and animals and went home.

"Cliffy, Cliffy bo biffy, banana fana fo fiffy, fee fi mo miffy, Cliffy!"

Woody stopped Keegan's stroller. It was a sunny, warm Monday morning. He was baby-sitting, following a very profitable weekend. Woody had earned nearly thirty dollars, just by selling his animals. And he had seen those three boys only once, on Saturday afternoon. (They had not seen Woody.) But now he recognized that voice. He looked up. Coming toward him on the boardwalk were the boys. The two younger ones were singing about the older one, whose name, apparently, was Cliffy.

The boys stopped singing when they recognized Woody.

"Hey!" cried Cliffy. "Hey, little mommy!"

"Shut up," said Woody.

"Da-da," added Keegan and drooled down his sunsuit.

"You're looking very cute today," one of the other boys said to Woody. "I like the bottle. The Three Little Pigs. Adorable."

Woody had stuck one of Keegan's bottles in the pocket of his jeans. It was decorated with small pink pigs. A baby blanket (known in the Rosso family as a "didey") was slung over one shoulder. Woody clenched his fists again. He stepped out from behind the stroller and advanced on the boys. Cliffy took a step backward.

"Ted!" he shouted. "Scott! Let's go!"

"Chicken!" Woody yelled after them.

"Barfburger!" Ted yelled back.

Woody narrowed his eyes.

Okay. This meant war. No one called Woody a barfburger and got away with it.

Woody took a vacation from his work. He set aside his stones and shells and pipe cleaners and glue. Then he snagged Hardy and asked him to do some sleuthing. Hardy did not need any encouragement. It wasn't often that he found good detective work.

"What do you want me to do, sir?" asked Hardy.

"Find out where those boys live," said Woody. He and Hardy were standing at the top of the steps to the beach. Woody was pointing to Cliffy, Ted, and Scott.

"No problem," replied Hardy. "Let me go get my detective equipment."

Woody wasn't sure what Hardy did that afternoon, but at dinnertime Hardy said, "Okay, Woodman, here's the scoop. The men in question are Clifford and Theodore Wallace and their cousin, Scott Hoban. They're here for a week—family vacation—and they're staying at fifteen Seahorse Walk. Clifford is eleven. Theodore and Scott are almost nine. Their hobby is teasing people. Any questions, sir?"

"Nope," replied Woody. "That was just what I needed to know."

The next morning, Woody got up early. He tiptoed into the living room. He found a piece of paper and a pen. He wrote some words in his best penmanship. He discovered that he was badly out of practice. So he made some neat letters and traced over them a few times. Then he took a fresh piece of paper and *very carefully* wrote:

Dear Mr. and Mrs. Wallace and Mr. and Mrs. Hoban, This is to inform you that your sons, Clifford and Theodore and Scott, are very bad pests. (Woody wanted to call them "nuisances," but he didn't know how to spell that.) *They have been teasing and tormenting all the kids around here in Davis Park. We suggest that you send them to their rooms. Sincerely,*

The Chief of the Davis Park Police Department

Several policemen did patrol Davis Park, although Woody was not sure there was an actual chief of police. He was hoping that the Wallaces and the Hobans would think there was, however. But Woody never found out what the adults thought. The next morning he was leaving Sandpiper House with a bag containing his paperweights and candy dishes and objets d'art when—

"Gotcha!"

Three figures jumped around a corner of the board-walk.

"Lay off!" shouted Woody.

"Jerk!" That was Cliffy. "We know you wrote that note. You are so lame." He swung at Woody, who dropped his bag. The bag landed on the walk with a crunch as nearly every shell inside cracked or broke.

Woody swung back. He missed Cliffy, but he hit Scott in the face.

He swung again.

Someone caught his arms from behind. "Give it a rest, Woody," said Bainbridge. He glared at Scott and his cousins. "And *you* get out of here."

Scott, Ted, and Cliffy ran down the boardwalk.

Bainbridge helped Woody back to Sandpiper House.

Mrs. Rosso grounded Woody for a day.

"But Cliffy—that other kid—he hit me first. I mean, he tried to," Woody complained to his mother. "And he made me drop my bag. Half my stuff is ruined. I bet that's about fifty bucks worth of, um, merchandise."

"You can spend the day making new things then," said Mrs. Rosso more gently. "The point is, you are *not* supposed to fight. Besides, it's a long trip from here to the emergency room."

"Okay, okay."

That afternoon, Woody was carefully gluing a shell

head onto a stone lion when Hardy burst into the house. "Hey, guess what!" exclaimed Hardy. (He didn't give Woody a chance to guess.) "I just found out that every summer on Labor Day weekend, there's this big crafts fair in Davis Park."

"So?" said Woody.

"So anyone who wants to can sell stuff at the fair. You just have to rent a table for the day, or something like that. Think of all the stuff you could sell, Woody. *Every*one goes to the fair."

"All *right*!" exclaimed Woody.

On Saturday, Scott and his relatives left Fire Island. They sailed off on an afternoon ferry.

Woody stood on the dock. "So long, suckers!" he yelled.

The boys didn't hear him.

Woody was glad he'd never have to see them again. But he sort of wished they could be around for the crafts fair to watch him earn a million dollars with his cute little froggies.

Woody headed for the store to buy himself a lobster hat.

8

Gardenia and the Movie on the Beach

"Pssst! Hey! Faustine! Today's the day!"

Faustine didn't move. She didn't even open her eyes. After several seconds she finally murmured, "What time is it, Dinnie?"

Gardenia turned on the light. "It's—"

"Ohhhh, Dinnie. That's killing my eyes. What are you *do*ing?"

"I thought you wanted to know what time it is."

"I do. But I thought it was morning, not the middle of the night."

Dinnie flicked off the light. "It *is* morning," she told her sister. "It's four-thirty. And today is the big day."

"Four-thirty," said Faustine, rolling over, "is still the middle of the night. Wake me when the sun is up." Faustine put her pillow over her head.

Dinnie yawned. She was wide awake. How could

anyone possibly sleep when she was just hours away from . . . her movie debut? Later that morning, the Rossos (all eleven kids) would have their big chance. They were finally going to get to be extras in a scene in Justin's movie.

Extras, Dinnie had learned, usually don't get to say anything unless they're all talking at once so you can't really understand them. But that was okay. The Rossos were needed to pose as kids in a beach scene in Justin's movie. They would appear in the background of the scene and they were supposed to do beachy things, like sit on blankets or build sand castles, while the camera focused on Justin and Chloe, who would be walking along the water's edge, having a serious talk about their relationship. A lot of other Fire Islanders, including Melanie and Lacey, were going to be beach extras, too. (Everybody would get paid.)

Dinnie lay in her bed. She wondered whether she would get to wear makeup. Or whether Laura would curl her hair the way she had curled Jan's. Ordinarily, Dinnie didn't care much about getting dressed up. But she thought she ought to look glamorous for her movie debut.

Dinnie lay in her bed for as long as she could stand it. Near six o'clock, she finally got up. She tiptoed into the living room, wondering how she was going to occupy herself until her brothers and sisters woke up. Dinnie discovered that she wasn't alone. Candy was up, too.

"It's movie day!" Dinnie whispered excitedly to Candy.

"I know!" Candy, who had seemed preoccupied nearly all summer, actually looked halfway normal that morning.

"I don't know how I can wait any longer. Oh, I hope I get a really good extra part. I hope I get to throw a Frisbee or do *some*thing so people will notice me. Maybe I could rescue a hurt dog."

"Yeah . . ." Now Candy was far away.

Dinnie followed her sister's gaze. She realized that Candy was staring out the window at (what else?) the house next door.

"Are you *still* thinking about that stupid house?" asked Dinnie impatiently.

"Mm-hmm."

"Candy, come *on*. There's no mystery. Or if there is, half of it's in your imagination. The other half is probably someone playing tricks. Hannah. Or Woody. Or even the special effects people with the movie. You've seen the kinds of things they can do. They're practically magicians."

"They can't give me weird dreams," said Candy.

"No . . ." Dinnie kept her opinion about her sister's dreams to herself. She didn't want to get into an argument on the day of her movie debut.

Several hours later the Rosso kids were up and dressed. Mrs. Rosso took care of dressing Keegan.

When she brought him into the living room, he looked like he was ready to have his school picture taken. He was wearing a freshly washed and ironed blue sunsuit, white socks, and a pair of white baby shoes. Although he had very little hair, Mrs. Rosso had combed what he did have and had even parted it and slicked it down with water.

"Mom! What have you done?" exclaimed Dinnie.

"Yeah, who *is* that?" asked Woody.

"It's your *brother*," said Mrs. Rosso.

"How'd he get to be forty-five years old?" asked Bainbridge.

"Mom, he's supposed to look like a beach baby," added Abbie. "He should be wearing bathing trunks and a T-shirt and his sunhat. And his hair should look the way it always does."

"Yeah," said Hannah. "You know, like he brushed it himself."

Mrs. Rosso sighed. She disappeared with Keegan. When she returned, Keegan was a baby again. He was even slobbering over a piece of pretzel.

"Okay, let's go!" cried Abbie. "Mel and Lacey are waiting." She stooped and picked up Keegan, shifting him so that he rested on her hip. "Are you sure you don't want to come, Mom?" asked Abbie. "They need grown-ups for this scene, too."

"I'll leave the acting to you kids," Mrs. Rosso replied. "Have fun."

Dinnie piled out of the house with her brothers and

sisters. She grabbed Faustine's arm. "May moo-vray le sacaray et le bon-bons?" she said.

"Oh, mais non. Le bon-bon et le sacaray fay le—"

"No French!" ordered Hannah.

"Yeah, cut it out, you guys," added Abbie. "I don't want you to make a fool of me in front of Justin and Chloe."

"Can we make a fool of you in front of Mel and Lacey?" asked Woody.

"No!" cried Abbie, but she was laughing.

"How much are we getting paid today?" asked Hardy. "I forgot."

"Fifty bucks," Abbie reminded him.

"Fifty bucks *each* for *each day* we work," said Ira.

"Maybe they will need us for ten days," said Jan. "Then I would earn . . ."

"Five hundred dollars!" exploded Woody, who was not much good at math unless there were dollar signs in front of the numbers.

Faustine sighed with pleasure. "If I had five hundred dollars, I would donate it to one of those places that helps hurt animals."

"I don't care how much money I earn. I just want to become a famous movie star," said Dinnie.

"Gardenia, you are going to be an *extra* today, and that's it," said Abbie.

"I know, I know, I know." But Dinnie was imagining something. It was a large poster. The poster was an ad for a movie. And across the top were capital letters that read: STARRING REGINA ROSSO. (Regina would be Gardenia's stage name. She would change it as soon as possible.) A crowd of people was exclaiming over the poster. They were saying, "What a brilliant star," and "Such talent!" and "A brilliant actress. She's the next Julia Roberts."

"There are Mel and Lacey!" called Abbie, in the middle of Dinnie's good daydream. "Hurry up, you guys."

Dinnie and her brothers and sisters raced down the beach to where Mel and Lacey were milling around with Timmy and Jackie (their younger brothers) and a *crowd* of people. There were men wearing sunglasses, women carrying towels and blankets, and children with books and kites and Frisbees.

"Are *all* these people going to be in the movie today?" Dinnie whispered to her twin. (She ducked as a Frisbee whizzed over her head.)

"I guess . . ." said Faustine slowly. "Quelle sombloovay. Je voudrais—"

"Shut up!" hissed Abbie. "No French! And yes, all these people are going to be in the movie today, Dinnie. It's a crowd scene, remember?"

"Yeah," mumbled Dinnie. She paused. "Abbie? Is being an extra going to be fun?"

Melanie answered for Abbie. "It's going to be *work*. And it might be boring."

Dinnie sagged. This was not what she had expected.

Unfortunately, Mel was right. All morning, the extras waited. The director kept saying, "Okay, beach crowd. It's time to—" And then something would go wrong. So the beach crowd sat. Or stood. Or talked. Keegan fussed, and Abbie had to take him home twice; once to change his diaper and once to get him a bottle of water. Ira had to go home a couple of times, too. He kept adding things to his outfit.

"You look like a mummy," said Hannah finally.

"Do you want me to get sunburned?" Ira retorted, which was an unfortunate choice of words because Hannah replied, "Oh, why not?"

It was past one o'clock in the afternoon when the director said to the extras, "*Now* we're ready. Do you understand what to do? In this scene, Justin and Chloe are walking by the water's edge, deep in serious conversation. You are simply the people on the beach doing whatever you'd be doing ordinarily—reading, playing, swimming, sunbathing. You are *not* paying attention to Justin and Chloe, okay? You don't know them. They're just two people walking down the beach. Don't even look at them."

The director and two others, a man and a woman, helped organize the extras. They handed out a few props. The woman gave Dinnie a plastic sand pail and shovel. She handed another pail and shovel to Faustine.

"You two are adorable," she said. "Stay together

and work on a sand castle right here, okay? Just play like you do everyday."

"Did you hear that?" Dinnie cried softly, as soon as the woman was out of earshot. "Faustine! She said I'm adorable."

"She said *we're* adorable. After all, we *are* identical," Faustine pointed out.

Dinnie wasn't listening. She was thinking: If I'm adorable, I should be noticed.

At long last, the beach scene was set up. Justin and Chloe began to walk along the water's edge, talking seriously.

Faustine dutifully concentrated on creating a sand castle. Dinnie tried to be helpful. But it was so hard not to watch Justin, Chloe, and the action. Dinnie halfheartedly dug at some sand. She waited until she saw a camera that she thought was directed at her. She grinned. Then she waved.

"Cut!" yelled the director. "Little girl, what are you doing? Please follow directions."

Justin and Chloe began the scene again. They were walking by the twins when Dinnie stood up, abandoning her shovel, and turned a cartwheel. (She landed on her bottom, but she didn't care.)

"Cut!" yelled the director. He ran to Dinnie. "Little girl," he said again. He sounded very angry. But he caught himself and said sweetly, "Little girl, your job is to *hold still*."

This time Dinnie followed them down the beach. She turned another cartwheel.

"Cut!" yelled the director. "Little girl, let me ask you one more time. *What are you doing?*"

"Acting," replied Dinnie.

"Dinnie—" began Justin.

"You know this kid?" said the director to Justin.

"Sort of," he replied. Abbie darted to Justin and whispered something to him. Justin frowned. Then he smiled. "She's an aspiring actress," he announced. He pulled the director aside and spoke to him for a few moments. The director sighed loudly. But he nodded his head. Justin called to Dinnie.

"Yeah?" Dinnie trotted over to Justin and the director.

"If I give you a small part to play in this scene, will you do it silently, follow directions and leave Justin and Chloe alone?" the director asked Dinnie sternly.

Dinnie gulped. "Yes," she managed to say.

"All right."

The director told Dinnie that she could take a dog for a walk and that she and the dog could pass right in front of the camera.

"All *right*!" exclaimed Dinnie. This was perfect. What an opportunity. She was going to make her acting debut with an *animal*.

The cameras began to roll again. Someone handed a leash to Dinnie (a fluffy gray dog was attached to the

end) and gave her a little push. Dinnie walked proudly
down the beach. She didn't grin or wave or turn a
cartwheel. She considered letting the dog loose and
then chasing after him but decided not to.

Justin and Chloe had nearly finished a mistake-free
scene when—

"Aughhh!" A shriek rang out.

"It wasn't me!" Dinnie yelled.

Everyone looked around frantically.

"It was me," said Candy in a trembly voice. "There's
a face at the window!"

"Oh, for heaven's sake!" muttered Abbie.

"A face at the window?" repeated Chloe, confused.

"Yes! Over there! In the empty house!"

Now everyone shaded their eyes and looked down
the beach.

"How can you see that far?" asked Justin.

"I just can," replied Candy in a small voice.

"So can I. And there's nothing at any window at
that house," snapped the director. "Everyone back to
work. We're wasting time. And money."

"You *goon*!" whispered Dinnie to Candy.

"You're the goon," replied Candy. "Don't you get
it? All the special effects people are *here*. So there must
be a ghost at the house. I've been telling you all summer that it's haunted."

"You!" cried the director, pointing to Candy.
"Out!"

Dinnie might have put up a fuss, but Candy just wandered away, her eyes glued to the house. (Her mind was probably glued to it, too.)

"All right. Positions, everybody. And no more mistakes!" The director said a very bad word then, and Dinnie and Faustine looked at each other and nearly exploded into giggles.

Luckily, Dinnie calmed down. The cameras rolled again. As Justin and Chloe said their lines, Dinnie walked the little dog, acting quite casual, as if she were in front of cameras every day.

The scene ended. For a moment, everyone was silent. Justin and Chloe glanced at each other, then at the director.

"It's a take!" the director announced.

Dinnie let out a cheer. "I'm going to be famous!" she cried. She ran to Justin. "Oh, thank you, thank you, thank you for giving me my big break."

"No problem," replied Justin, grinning.

Someday, thought Dinnie, the whole world would know about Regina Rosso.

9

Bainbridge and the Case of the Curious Kidnapping

One morning, late in August, Bainbridge lay in his bed, waking slowly and realizing that he was cold. All summer long, he had found his bedroom stuffy and hot in the morning, and sometimes at night, too. Now he needed the extra blanket that was folded across the foot of his bed.

It must be raining, thought Bainbridge. Great. Only five days of freedom left before we leave the island and go back to school, and one of them is going to be wasted indoors. What a drag.

But when Bainbridge raised the shade and looked outside, he saw a bright, sunny day. Shivering, he got up and pulled on a T-shirt. Then he stepped into the living room, whispered a good morning to his mother and Candy, who were sitting in the kitchen, and opened the front door.

He breathed in deeply. The air was beachy—salty and sharp—but it was chilly. Bainbridge noticed a few red leaves on the sumac bushes. It's almost fall, he realized. Summer is ending.

Bainbridge had thoroughly enjoyed the summer. He was somewhat worried about Candy, who might possibly be looney tunes or going bonkers, he thought. Other than that, life was great. For one thing, Bainbridge had met Amelia on the beach. His chick-watching had paid off, although now that he and Amelia were spending so much time together, Bainbridge no longer thought of her as a chick. Amelia was his friend. And he hoped he was hers.

For another thing, the crafts fair would be held the next day—Saturday. Bainbridge was eager to see how Woody would do. His younger brother had signed up for a table at the fair and had created a menagerie of animals to sell, along with a selection of candy dishes and his new line of soap dishes. (Like the candy dishes, the soap dishes were decorated clamshells. Bainbridge couldn't distinguish the two kinds of dishes, but apparently Woody could.)

Bainbridge had high hopes for the last days of his vacation. He and Amelia would spend most of their time together. They would sunbathe on the beach, walk through the wildlife preserve, buy ice-cream cones, help Woody at the fair, play volleyball, and maybe do a little body-surfing.

But Bainbridge's plans began to fall apart right after breakfast that morning—when Amelia showed up.

She knocked on the screen door. Hardy dashed to it, let Amelia in, and called, "Hey, Bainbridge, your girl friend is here."

Bainbridge rarely lost his temper. He was so good-natured that kids hardly ever teased him, even about his name (unlike hot-tempered Dagwood, who was often teased because kids knew they could get a rise out of him).

Bainbridge ignored the "girl friend" remark. Possibly, he hadn't noticed it. At any rate (to Hardy's dismay), Bainbridge merely walked to the door, calling, "Hey, Amelia. You're up early."

"We got bad news last night," she whispered. "Bainbridge? Can I talk to you in private? It's sort of important."

"Let's sit outside," Bainbridge replied. Then he added, "Away from the windows." (He knew his brothers and sisters too well.)

Bainbridge and Amelia walked to the top of the steps that led to the beach.

"What's wrong?" asked Bainbridge, putting his arm around Amelia.

"My grandfather called last night. Grandma Joan had a heart attack. It was a mild one, but she's in the hospital, and my dad wants to see her right away. So we have to leave. We're flying to Arizona this afternoon."

Bainbridge could feel his stomach drop. "You have to leave?" he repeated.

Amelia nodded.

So Bainbridge and Amelia said good-bye. Bainbridge wasn't sure if he'd see her again. He lived in New Jersey; she lived in Connecticut. And Bainbridge didn't know whether his family would return to Fire Island the next summer.

"Are you still going to help me tomorrow?" Woody asked Bainbridge that evening. "You don't have to—"

"Don't you want me to?" replied Bainbridge.

"Yeah, but—"

"Then I'll be there. I've been looking forward to the fair."

"Me, too."

Bainbridge and Woody woke up extra early on Saturday morning.

"I'm never the first one up," commented Woody sleepily.

"Me neither," mumbled Bainbridge. "But come on. The fair is going to start in a few hours. You have a lot to do."

So did Bainbridge. However, just as he and Woody were about to set off for the fair, Mrs. Rosso called, "Bainbridge? I need you to watch Keegan this morning."

Bainbridge groaned. But he knew better than to protest. "You do?" he said.

His mother nodded. "Your father and I want to pack up some of this stuff. We may even mail a few cartons home so we don't have to wedge them into the van. We seem to have acquired an awful lot of junk this summer. By the way, do you know if Ira wants his *entire* shell collection? Some of it is getting smelly."

"I don't know," Bainbridge replied. He set Keegan in the stroller and tied on his little sneakers with the anchors printed over the toes. Then he packed up the diaper bag and called to Woody.

"Yeah?" his brother called back.

"Why don't you go on ahead? I'll come in a few minutes. Keegan isn't quite ready to leave. You know."

"Oh. Stinky diaper?" said Woody.

"Very," Bainbridge answered.

"See you later!" Woody flew out of the beach house, leaving Bainbridge to deal with the mess Keegan had created. And it was a spectacular mess. Bainbridge had to remove every article of Keegan's clothing and replace it. Even the anchor sneakers. When they left the house, Keegan was dressed in a Mickey Mouse T-shirt, plaid shorts, green knee socks, and sandals. (Mrs. Rosso frowned at the sight but didn't say anything.)

Bainbridge raced Keegan's stroller bumpily along the boardwalks between his house and the church in which the crafts fair was held. (The church, located not far from Bedside Manor, was called Our Lady of the Most Precious Blood. It was the only church in Davis Park and Ocean Ridge.)

When Bainbridge reached the fair, he paused at the doorway of the church to examine a display of tiny paintings of seascapes. Each one was no more than two inches wide by two inches tall, and each came in its own small frame. Next to the paintings was a rack of handmade jewelry. Beyond that was a table piled with brightly colored handbags, duffel bags, and carryalls.

Bainbridge wheeled Keegan into the church. With the crafts fair bustling, the church didn't look much like a church. It looked more like a mall. Tables and stalls were jammed into every inch of the building. Signs read: "Special Two-for-One Sale" and "Finest Quality" and "Low, Low Price." People crowded the pathways between the displays. Children ran and shouted.

Bainbridge wasn't terribly interested in crafts, but he was interested in seeing how some of the craftspeople worked. He watched a young girl tying flies for fishing. He watched a man sketch a caricature of a little boy. And then he came to a stand draped with flashy T-shirts. More T-shirts were stacked behind it. Bainbridge reached for a bright red and yellow shirt with the words "Davis Park" scrawled under a painting of a sunset.

"Cool," he murmured. He checked the size. The shirt was too big, so he put it back.

"Like that one?" asked a young woman from behind the table. Bainbridge hadn't even noticed her. She was about his age, tall and slim, with wispy brown hair. Bainbridge decided she was the most beautiful girl he'd ever seen. (Not counting Amelia, of course.)

"Sure," replied Bainbridge. "But it's not my size."

"Let me make another one for you then," said the girl. "What size are you?"

"Medium. . . . You're going to *make* the T-shirt?"

"Why not? I made all these." The girl indicated the stacks of T-shirts piled around her. "I've been doing this for years."

"How do you paint on fabric?" asked Bainbridge.

"*I* use a spray gun. Other people do different things."

Bainbridge watched her spray a complicated scene onto the front of a T-shirt. "Excuse me, but what's your name?" he asked.

"Blaire. What's yours?"

"Bainbridge," said Bainbridge.

"And I thought *my* name was weird."

Bainbridge and Blaire began to talk. Bainbridge felt somewhat guilty about being so friendly with Blaire while Amelia was at her grandparents' house trying to help her grandfather. But he couldn't ignore the fact that he liked Blaire.

After a few minutes, Blaire spread her new masterpiece on the counter. "It's all yours," she said.

"How much?"

"No charge. It's a present."

"Thanks! Hey, what are you going to do after the fair closes today?"

Blaire shrugged. "Not sure."

"Do you like babies?" asked Bainbridge.

"I guess," Blaire answered. "Why?"

"Want to meet my little brother?"

"Well . . . sure. But not right now. I don't want to leave the fair. Can I meet him tomorrow or something?" Blaire removed a small white T-shirt from a pile on a table behind her. She spread it out and smoothed away the wrinkles. "I'll paint this one for your brother," she added. "What's his name? Does he like ducks?"

Bainbridge smiled. "He loves ducks. And his name is Keegan."

"Keegan! Another, um, unusual name."

"Oh, we all have unusual names."

"All?"

"There are eleven of us. Plus our parents. My mother named us in alphabetical order. Abigail, Bainbridge, Calandra . . ." Bainbridge completed the list. Then, in order to extend his conversation with Blaire, he told her about Zsa-Zsa. And about his parents. "See, my mom has this thing about systems—"

"Excuse me," said an impatient voice. "I'd like a T-shirt."

"And my dad," Bainbridge continued. "Well, he—"

"Ahem."

A line was forming next to Bainbridge.

"I've got customers," Blaire whispered hoarsely. "Give me your address and I'll come over tonight to meet Keegan."

"Hey! You don't have to wait until then," said Bainbridge.

"Bainbridge—"

"Come on, Cambridge," said the man at his elbow.

Bainbridge ignored him. "You can meet Keegan now," he told Blaire. "He's right— He's right— Hey, where is he?"

Bainbridge's stomach flip-flopped. He had turned around and discovered that Keegan and the stroller were gone. Or at any rate, they weren't where Bainbridge had last seen them. They couldn't be *gone*, though. Someone had probably jostled the stroller and it had rolled off.

"Oh no!" Bainbridge craned his neck around. The inside of Our Lady of the Most Precious Blood was teeming with people. He couldn't see past the ones who were crowded around him. "Get me a chair!" shouted Bainbridge.

"What?" cried Blaire.

"A chair! I need a chair! Give me your chair!" Bainbridge reached across the table for a folding chair piled with T-shirts. He swept the shirts away and hauled the chair toward him.

"Now just a minute, Cambridge," said the man.

"My name is Bainbridge." Bainbridge had set the chair down and was standing on it. From his new vantage point he could see dozens of strollers. But none of them was Keegan's. He glanced down.

Blaire was looking up at him. "What *are* you doing?" she asked.

"Keegan is gone. My brother is *gone*!"

"Who's gone?" asked the man. "Mr. Cougan?"

"Keegan! Keegan!" shouted Bainbridge.

"His baby brother," added Blaire. Now she looked concerned. The next thing Bainbridge knew, Blaire had crawled under her table and was standing by the chair. "*Help!*" she screamed.

Everywhere heads turned. Eyes fell on Bainbridge since he was still standing on the chair and was therefore more visible than anyone else.

"What is it? What's wrong?" Abbie, Candy, Hardy, Faustine, and Dinnie ran up to the chair. They had just arrived at the fair.

"Keegan's gone!" exclaimed Bainbridge. "Spread out and search!"

"Gone?" repeated Abbie.

"Gone. His stroller, too."

"The baby is gone. Stroller and all," murmured Candy, but no one heard her. And no one noticed when she slipped out of Our Lady of the Most Precious Blood and paused a little distance away, looking in the direction of the unnamed tumbledown house.

Inside the church, the Rosso kids frantically decided on a plan of attack, Bainbridge taking charge. "One, don't tell Mom or Dad yet," he said, out of breath. "Two, split up and start looking. Half of you guys look outdoors. The rest of you look in here."

"What about me?" Woody called from his stand.

"Stay there for now!" barked Bainbridge. "We'll call you if we need you."

Bainbridge jumped off the chair. He ran through the crowd, calling, "Keegan! Keegan! Where are you?"

"Like he's really going to answer," muttered Hardy.

Bainbridge's heart was pounding. He felt as if he might throw up. When he saw Abbie burst back inside the church from her brief search outdoors, he ran to her. He knew it was time to tell an adult what had happened, and he wanted Abbie to do it.

"I found him!" Abbie shrieked. "I found him!"

"Oh, thank goodness." The muscles in Bainbridge's body felt like wet spaghetti.

"He's with Hannah."

Abbie, Bainbridge, and Faustine dashed out of the church and joined Dinnie, Hardy, and Candy, standing together on the boardwalk, staring at Hannah. Hannah was a little distance down the walk, wheeling Keegan along slowly. Well, she wasn't exactly wheeling him.

"The stroller is moving by itself!" cried Candy.

"Oh, my gosh. It *is*," whispered Abbie.

Bainbridge jumped. Then he calmed down. "The boardwalk must be on a hill," he said. He looked at Hannah. "What are you doing?" he yelled. "We thought Keegan had been kidnapped. How could you be so—"

Hannah's eyes filled with tears. She grasped the stroller and wheeled it to Bainbridge's feet. (Candy's eyes were still the size of hubcaps.) "Nobody was paying attention to Keegan," said Hannah, and sniffled. "You were busy talking to that girl. So I took him for a walk."

"Well, don't ever do that again!" said Abbie.

Bainbridge left Abbie to yell at Hannah. He dashed back inside Our Lady of the Most Precious Blood, told Woody and Blaire that Keegan had been found safe and sound, and then returned to his little brother. As the eldest boy (and also the one who had been left in charge of Keegan), Bainbridge felt it was his duty to inform his parents of the accident—now that it was over and everything had turned out all right.

Accompanied by Candy and Hannah, Bainbridge wheeled Keegan back to Sandpiper House. (His other brothers and sisters returned to the fair to watch Woody's progress.)

"Mom," said Bainbridge. "Dad. I have to tell you something."

Mrs. Rosso finished packing folded sheets into a cardboard carton. Mr. Rosso turned away from the refrigerator, which he was cleaning out. "Yes?" they said, looking preoccupied.

"Um, we had a little problem with Keegan," Bainbridge began.

His parents glanced at the baby. "He looks all right," said Mrs. Rosso. "Except for that horrible outfit he's wearing."

Bainbridge explained what had happened. "I'm really sorry," he said when he had finished. "*Really* sorry. I promise I'll never be so irresponsible again." Bainbridge studied his parents' faces. Was he the next kid to be grounded? "You can ground me, if you want," he added. "I guess I deserve it."

"I don't think that will be necessary," his father replied. "You already feel bad enough."

A little while later, Bainbridge returned to the crafts fair with Keegan. As he walked along, he began to feel guilty about Amelia. If he'd been true to Amelia, this would not have happened.

Bainbridge decided to call her as soon as his family returned to New Jersey. He needed to talk to her.

10

Eberhard and the House of the Cursed

Hardy was sitting on a rock at the edge of the bay, thinking about Hannah. He had been present when Abbie had spotted Hannah with Keegan and the stroller. Hardy had noticed a smug smile on Hannah's face as the stroller seemed to wheel itself along the boardwalk. His younger sister was up to something, and Hardy (the detective) planned to find out what. He thought there was more to Keegan's "kidnapping" than Hannah had admitted, yet she had taken no blame for the crime. Hardy felt a sleuthey duty to clear up this mystery. It was his job to solve The Case of the Curious Kidnapping.

"What are you doing?"

Hardy jumped. The voice was right in his ear, but he had not heard anyone approach. He swiveled his head around. "Candy!" he exclaimed.

"Sorry if I scared you," Candy muttered. She plopped down in the sand. "Hardy?" she said after a moment.

"Yeah?"

"I need to hire you. I need you to solve a mystery." Candy had hired Hardy once before, to help her locate a secret passage on their farm in New Jersey. Hardy hadn't been much help, but now Candy was desperate.

Hardy straightened up. "You need a detective, ma'am?" he said.

Candy nodded (and sighed).

"What seems to be the trouble?" asked Hardy.

"It's the ghosts. You know, the haunted house next door. I just *have* to know what's going on. I wanted to solve the mystery myself, but I don't think I can. I've been haunted by those ghosts all summer. And I think that this morning, one of them made Hannah take Keegan. I don't care what anyone says: Something is going on. And it isn't funny, and I'm not crazy. But I will be crazy if we leave the island and I don't know what was happening next door." Candy looked as if she might cry.

"Hmm," murmured Hardy. He stroked his chin. "That's tough." He had wanted simply to find out more about Keegan's "kidnapping." But Candy was asking him to solve that and a lot more.

"You're a good detective!" exclaimed Candy. "And anyway you're the *only* detective I know of."

"Oh, I could solve your case, ma'am," Hardy assured his sister. "That's not the problem, of course. The problem is I'm not sure I have enough time to solve it before we go home. I mean, I may be a genius, but I'm not Superman."

"But you're my only hope!" wailed Candy. "Come on. What's your fee? I'll pay you anything."

Hardy frowned. Candy drove a tough bargain. "I'll cut you a deal," he said finally.

"Anything," said Candy. "Anything within reason, that is. I can't pay you a million dollars. In fact, I can't pay you more than twelve dollars."

"Twelve dollars, then," said Hardy.

"All twelve?" shrieked Candy.

"I thought you wanted me to solve your case."

"We-ell . . ."

"How about this? Twelve bucks if I solve the mystery before we go home. If I *don't* solve it in time, no charge."

"Okay," Candy replied slowly. "It's a deal."

Back at Sandpiper House, Hardy set to work. His first task was to make out a contract and ask Candy to sign it.

"How come?" asked Candy impatiently.

"If I solve this mystery, I want to be sure you pay up. I don't work for free."

"Okay, okay, okay." Candy signed her name on the

line Hardy had drawn at the bottom of the paper. Then she said, "Finished! What do we do first?"

"I make a phone call, and you help Mom pack."

"What's packing got to do with detecting?" asked Candy.

"Nothing. I work alone, that's all. As well as for pay," added Hardy. He watched Candy stalk into his parents' bedroom. Then he sat down by the telephone with a pencil and a pad of paper. He had no phone directory, however, so he had to place several calls before he learned the number of the public library on the mainland.

"Great!" Hardy congratulated himself. He would not be able to go to the library, he knew, but he could ask the librarian a few questions. He just needed to find out some local history.

Hardy dialed the number. The phone rang once and was picked up right away. "Hello!" cried Hardy. "Can you please—"

"Hello," replied the recorded message at the other end of the line. "You have reached the John Adams Memorial Library. We are closed for Labor Day weekend. We will reopen on—"

It didn't matter when the library would reopen. It would be too late. Hardy needed answers to his questions before the weekend was over. So he hung up the phone, the message still playing.

A good detective doesn't give up, Hardy reminded

himself. Especially if giving up means he won't get paid.

Hardy reviewed what he knew about the house next door, which wasn't much. He thought he remembered finding out that no one had lived in the house for at least twenty years. Now how did he know that?

I need my detecting hat, Hardy thought. Luckily, he had brought it to Fire Island. When he had first packed it, on the farm in New Jersey, his mother had frowned. Later, she had removed it from his suitcase. That was when she had decided that the Rossos had overpacked for the summer and she was frantically weeding out everything she felt was unnecessary. Hardy had convinced her he needed the hat. "Besides," he'd pointed out, "you're letting Jan bring along that disgusting jar full of those old brown baby teeth she lost."

So the hat came along. Hardy put it on his head. "I knew you'd come in handy," he told the hat. (This was the second time he'd needed it that summer.)

Hardy and his hat left Sandpiper House. Hardy was carrying a notepad, a pencil, and his magnifying glass. He walked to the beach. Then he walked to an empty stretch of sand and sat down. Let's see, he thought. What should I do to crack this case? Hmm. A good detective hunts for clues with his magnifying glass. He interviews suspects. He gathers information.

Twenty years. The house had been deserted for twenty years. Who had said that? It was Candy,

Hardy answered himself. But how had she known that? Had she made it up? Noooo . . .

Then Hardy remembered. Candy had heard it from Mel or Lacey. They ought to know. Their parents had been summering on Fire Island forever. They were old-timers.

"That's it!" Hardy cried. "I'll talk to old-timers." He would start with the parents of Mel and Lacey. Then he would talk to those fishermen the twins had been pestering. Maybe they would know other people he should talk to. Hardy jumped to his feet.

Holding his hat in place with one hand and clutching his notebook in his other, Hardy ran down the beach. He ran past Justin and Chloe, rehearsing a scene for *Summer Blues*. He ran past Jan and Ira, building an elaborate castle at the water's edge. By the time he reached the stairs to the boardwalk, he had not seen Mel or Lacey or anyone in their families. He wasn't surprised, though. The sunny day had turned cloudy, and anyway a lot of people were at the church looking around the crafts fair.

Hardy trotted straight to the Bradermans' house. He found Melanie perched on the railing, eating a peach and staring into space. Her expression changed when she saw Hardy. "Hey!" she called. "Hi. How are you? What's with the hat?"

"I have an important mystery to solve. May I have a moment of your time, ma'am?"

Mel hopped off the railing. She stood at attention. "Yes, sir?"

"Ma'am, how long have you been coming to Fire Island?"

"Since I was a baby, sir."

"How about your parents?"

"Around twenty years, sir."

"Are they home?"

"Mrs. Braderman is."

Hardy narrowed his eyes. "You call your mother Mrs. Braderman?"

"No, but you should."

Hardy detected a smile on Mel's lips. He ignored it. A good detective sticks to his business. "May I talk to her, ma'am?" he asked.

Mel ushered Hardy inside the beach house.

"Just a few questions, ma— I mean, Mrs. Braderman," he said. Hardy described the unnamed house next door to Sandpiper. "Do you know it?"

Mrs. Braderman nodded. "Yes, but not well."

"Do you know how long it's been empty?"

"Years. This is my twentieth summer in Davis Park, and the house hasn't been lived in, as far as I know."

"Why?"

Mrs. Braderman pursed her lips. "Isn't that funny? I'm not sure why."

Most people, thought Hardy, would have considered this particular interview a waste of time. Not Hardy. He'd noted Mrs. Braderman's confusion when he'd asked why the house was empty. That was an important reaction. It must mean something. Hardy would think it over later. For now, he wrote in his notebook: *Mrs. Braderman thinks it's strange that the weird house has been empty but not torn down or anything*.

"Thank you, ma'am," said Hardy. He tipped his detective hat. Then he returned to the front deck. "Are Mr. and Mrs. Reeder home?" he asked Mel.

"Lacey's parents? I don't think so. They're probably at the fair. Or maybe the store. Or maybe walking on the beach."

Hardy decided to look for them later. He ambled back toward Sandpiper House, thinking that possibly Candy wasn't entirely crazy after all. He didn't know why she was being haunted by ghosts, but an empty beach house *was* sort of odd.

Hardy's sleuthing was interrupted when he caught sight of Hannah coming toward him along the walk. She hadn't noticed him yet, but she was smiling anyway. Just smiling to herself.

His sister glanced up then. "Hey, Hardy!" she yelled. "Come to the bay with me! A seaplane is about to land."

Hardy turned around. He followed Hannah to the bay.

Early the next morning, Hardy returned to his job. He had very little time in which to solve Candy's mystery and earn his twelve dollars. And he wanted the twelve dollars badly since Woody had earned over sixty at the fair the day before. Hardy was envious.

Hardy peeked into his notebook. The instruction "Talk to the parents of Mel and Lacey" was checked off (even though he had spoken only to Mrs. Braderman). Under that was written "Talk to the fishermen." That would be the perfect way to start Day Two of his sleuthing, Hardy decided.

Hardy dressed quietly and slipped out of his slumbering house. He ran down the beach to the spot where the three men were fishing, as they'd been doing almost every morning of the summer. One of them, the one who fished sitting down, saw Hardy before the other two did.

"Uh-oh. Here comes trouble," he muttered.

No wonder. The three men knew Faustine and Dinnie quite well by then, and they recognized the rest of the Rossos.

Hardy heard the comment. But it didn't stop him. "Good morning, sir," he began. "Detective Rosso here. I'd like to ask you a few questions."

The fisherman glanced at his friends. "Aye, aye," he said. "Go to it."

"Sir, how old are you?" asked Hardy.

"None of your—" the man began to say angrily. Then he paused. "I don't see why you'd want to know, but I'm sixty-seven."

Ooh, a *real* old-timer, thought Hardy. "Perfect," he

said. "Sir, are you familiar with the abandoned house next to ours? Next to Sandpiper?"

"House of the Cursed?"

Hardy blinked his eyes. "Is that what it's called?"

"Uh, yeah, sure," said the fisherman.

"What he means," added one of his friends (he was growing a stubbly white beard), "is that the house has been empty for so long, we'd almost forgotten its name."

"Right," agreed the third fisherman. "It's been empty for more than twenty-five years. Ever since the—the—"

"Ever since the tragedy," supplied the third fisherman.

"What tragedy?" whispered Hardy, and then he remembered to add, "Sir?"

"You don't know about it?" said the bearded man.

"It was before my time, sir," replied Hardy.

"Tell him the story, Ron," said the first fisherman, who was still seated in his beach chair. "And don't leave anything out."

Ron stroked his beard. "Well," he said. He looked at Hardy. "You got a minute, son?" (Hardy nodded.) "All right. It was twenty-five, no twenty-seven years ago. The day was bright and sunny but cool. Just like today." (Hardy shivered.) "Living in House of the Cursed was the Handiforth family—a young couple and their baby boy, Greer. Greer was about a year old." (Not much older than Keegan, thought Hardy.) "Course, way back then, it wasn't called House of the Cursed," Ron went on. "It was called Blue Skies House. Anyway, the Handiforths were a happy family. Mr. and Mrs. H. were very much in love, and they adored Greer. They felt lucky to be able to spend every summer on the island in the house they had built themselves.

"One day in early June, the Handiforths decided to go out in their boat, so they packed some food and set sail. But very quickly the blue sky was filled with dark, angry clouds. A squall had blown in, and the Handiforths' sailboat capsized. Mrs. Handiforth and Greer disappeared. Their bodies were never found, but it's pretty certain that they drowned. Mr. Handiforth was rescued, though. He was taken to a hospital to recover, and then he returned to Blue Skies House. But there he slowly went mad. He said he couldn't live without his wife and son. And sure enough, by the end of the summer, he was dead. Some say he died of a broken heart. That was when the house became known as House of the Cursed. No one has lived in it since Mr. Handiforth died."

Ron stopped speaking.

Hardy simply stared at him. After a moment, he murmured, "Oh my gosh." Then he ran all the way back to Sandpiper House.

*   *   *

"Do you swear this is true?" whispered Candy. She and Hardy were holed up in her bedroom. Hardy had just told her the incredible tale of the Handiforths.

"I told you the story exactly the way Ron told it to me," Hardy replied.

"Then that explains everything!" cried Candy. "There *are* spirits and strange phenomena. The house is haunted by the spirit of Mr. Handiforth. And maybe by the spirits of his wife and baby. Mr. Handiforth is mourning for his dead family. Remember those dreams I had? The drowning one must have been about Mrs. Handiforth and Greer. And the graveyard one must have been about their funeral. . . . Oh! And Keegan!When he disappeared yesterday, I bet the ghost of Mr. Handiforth was trying to get his baby boy back! He wants Greer really badly, but he doesn't know where he is. So he took Keegan instead. And— and the shells and the water and everything? You know, the stuff that would appear at night? I bet Mr. Handiforth wanted me to experience the squall. The rain and the storm . . . everything stirred up on the ocean floor. He wanted me to be scared just like— Yikes!" Candy shrieked. Then she lowered her voice. "I sense a presence in this room."

"It's me, stupid."

Hardy jumped a mile. Standing in the doorway was Hannah. Hardy noticed the funny smile on her lips. The smile grew until Hannah burst out laughing.

"You guys," she said, gasping. "You guys fell for everything!"

Hardy narrowed his eyes. "What?" he said.

"There's no ghost. I did everything, Candy. I've been tricking you all summer! I moaned outside your window, I sprayed the sill with water, I left the things in your room, I pushed Keegan's stroller down a little hill yesterday. And I—"

"Hannah Rosso!" boomed Mr. Rosso's voice.

"Uh-oh," muttered Hannah.

"Is this true? Have you been tormenting your sister all summer?"

"Yes. I mean, no. I wasn't tormenting her. I was just playing jokes. I needed something to do. Everybody was busy with*out* me."

Embarrassed as he was, Hardy had to hand it to Hannah. She had pulled off an incredible prank. It was the longest-lasting prank in Rosso history.

Candy looked mortified. "You mean you made those fishermen go along with your joke? They were making fun of me, too?"

"Oh, the fishermen don't have anything to do with this," Hannah answered. "They tell that story to lots of kids. They told it to me way back at the beginning of the summer. That's how I got the idea to trick you."

"You are in major trouble, young lady," Mr. Rosso said to Hannah.

*　　*　　*

And she was. Hannah was grounded for two weeks—starting on Fire Island. She wasn't permitted to leave Sandpiper House. When the Rossos would return to New Jersey, Hannah would be confined to her room, except to go to school.

"That was some joke, wasn't it?" Hardy said to Bainbridge the night of Hannah's confession. (Bainbridge nodded.) "But I feel kind of sorry for Candy. I don't think she'll ever speak to Hannah again. At least we know she's not crazy."

"I feel bad for her, too," replied Bainbridge, "but I also feel bad for Hannah. I guess we do kind of leave her out of things."

"Because she's always playing tricks!" exploded Hardy.

"She plays tricks because we leave her out!"

"She plays tricks because she's a jerk," said Candy's voice. She joined her brothers on the deck. "Hannah thinks she's so cool. She thinks she pulled off this big—this big scam. But she's not so clever. She couldn't make a curtain move in the window of House of the Cursed. She couldn't give me those bad dreams. I really was haunted by ghosts this summer."

Bainbridge rolled his eyes.

Hardy exclaimed, "Hey! You owe me twelve bucks. I solved your case."

"You did not," said Candy. "Hannah confessed."

"But I found out the ghost story for you."

"I'll pay you six dollars," Candy replied. "That's my final offer."

"I'll take it," said Hardy. He held out his hand. "Pay up."

Candy handed over the money to her brother, the detective, and Hardy stuffed it in his pocket. He was six dollars richer. Not bad.

Much later, Hardy lay in his bed, listening to the rush of the ocean waves. Sandpiper House was silent. In two days, the Rossos would leave the island and return to New Jersey. Hardy congratulated himself on having solved another mystery.

But something nagged at Hardy's practical mind. The ghost . . . the haunting. Candy had *said* that unexplainable things happen. And she seemed to be right. He had a little more respect for Candy now. But he hated to admit that he couldn't explain everything.

11

Keegan and the End of Summer

Keegan was bumping along. It seemed he was often bumping along. He bumped along in his stroller. (The boardwalks on Fire Island were especially bumpy.) Sometimes he bumped along on his father's shoulders. Or he bumped along in his mother's arms, or in his carseat. This bumping was different, though. It was bumping *and rolling*.

Keegan was riding on the *Kiki*. The crowded ferry chugged across the bay from Davis Park to Patchogue on the mainland. It carried Keegan, his parents, his brothers and sisters, Zsa-Zsa, the Rossos' summer belongings, and a lot of other people with *their* summer belongings.

From his seat in his sister's arms, Keegan gazed wide-eyed around the ferry. Already, Sandpiper

House was just a dim memory. And Keegan had no memory whatsoever of the farmhouse in New Jersey, although he would recognize it as soon as his family reached it that afternoon.

"Summer's over. It's all over," Dinnie was saying to Faustine. "No more summer."

"Yeah, back to school," grumbled Woody.

"Back to homework," added Hannah.

"You won't have any excuse for not doing yours, at least for the next two weeks," Candy said smugly to Hannah.

Hannah stuck out her tongue, which made Keegan laugh. So Hannah stuck out her tongue even farther, flared her nostrils, and rolled down her eyeballs so that only the whites of her eyes showed.

"Hannah!" hissed Abbie. Keegan swiveled around to look at his oldest sister. He was sitting in her lap, and he could tell something was wrong. Abbie's arms had stiffened. "Look normal!" Abbie ordered in a gruff whisper. "People are staring as it is."

"Well, no wonder," replied Hannah loudly. "They've probably never seen eleven orphans coming home from summer camp before." Hannah pretended to pout. "What a shame. Our wonderful, wonderful summer at the beach is over. Now we have to go back to the orphanage. Gosh. I sure hope someone adopts me soon. I want a home. . . . 'The sun'll come out tomorrow!' " she sang. " 'Bet your bottom dollar that—' *Oof!*"

Bainbridge had elbowed Hannah. "Shut up," he said. "People *are* staring. And anyway, how would you feel if you really *were* an orphan?"

"*I* would hope zat my French relatives would find me," Dinnie replied wickedly. She turned to Faustine. "Va voo salay le chat de la ploo?"

"Non, non, non. Je voudrais seulment le Chevrolet coupay."

"*Mrow!*" cried Zsa-Zsa.

"You're all terrible." Abbie hung her head. Then she whispered loudly to Mrs. Rosso, "Mom, I can't take it any longer. I'm moving over there." Abbie pointed to a space on a bench near the back of the ferry. "I'll take Keegan with me."

"All right," answered her mother, who was sitting with Jan—who was seasick and about to throw up into a garbage bag. (All the more reason, thought Abbie, to leave the immediate vicinity.)

The bumping increased as Abbie stood up and joggled Keegan against her shoulder. Then she managed to cross the ferry. She sat down by a window. "Look. Look out there, Keegan. See the waves? Hey, there's a seagull!"

Keegan didn't look out the window, though. He was busy watching his sister's face. Watching her mouth move and listening to the sounds that tumbled out of it. He had caught a familiar word. *Keegan*.

"Well," said Abbie, holding tightly to her baby brother, "we're on our way home. It's almost autumn again. What a summer we had. We made new friends. I made friends with Justin Hart, of all people. Bainbridge found a girl friend. And just possibly he learned not to be such a flirt with the 'chicks.' Keegan, don't *ever* refer to girls as 'chicks,' okay? Let's see. Candy starred in a ghost story. At least, I think she did. I'm not quite sure what happened to her. Let's just hope that if she really was haunted by a ghost or a poltergeist, it won't come home with her. Woody managed to earn a lot of money. Maybe there's hope for him after all. Maybe he'll be an entrepreneur someday."

Abbie kissed the top of Keegan's head. "I know you don't understand what I'm saying, but you look as if you're listening. And you aren't barfing or meowing or speaking fake French, which is good.

"Hardy solved some mysteries," Abbie continued. "He usually does. Faustine made a pest of herself with the fishermen, but she also made her point about cruelty to animals. Dinnie made her movie debut. I can't wait to see that film. When you're older, Keegan, I'll rent the movie, and I'll wait for our beach scene, and then I'll point you out and say, 'Keegan, that's you! That's Fire Island. Can you believe you were ever that little?' I'll have to say that. Grown-ups *always* say that to kids.

"Hannah . . . well, I keep thinking Hannah's going to learn a lesson from her practical jokes. You know, like, *don't play any*. People just get mad at you. But she keeps playing them. Maybe when she's done being grounded, I'll spend more time with her. Maybe that will help.

"Ira got sick, but he recovered. And Jan got beautiful. Remember her beauty treatment, Keegan? And what about you? What did you do this summer? You crawled around a lot. You pulled Zsa-Zsa's tail. You went for walks in your stroller. Not too different from being at home, I guess."

Abbie's voice was a pleasant hum in Keegan's ears. He allowed his eyes to close, the boat rocking beneath him, his sister's arms encircling him safely. He drifted off to sleep.

Keegan awoke when Abbie announced, "Here we are!" and stood up.

There was lots of bustle and movement as everyone else stood up too and began crowding toward the *Kiki*'s doors.

"Who's got Zsa-Zsa?" called Mrs. Rosso.

"Mommy, I still don't feel good," said Jan.

"Moi, je suis tres, tres beau," said Dinnie.

"My sunburn hurts," said Ira.

"Roll around in butter," Woody suggested.

"Oh, are we here?" Mr. Rosso tore his eyes away from a carpentry magazine and glanced around dazedly.

"We're here, Dad," Abbie replied. "Come on. Let's go."

Abbie counted heads. Mom, Dad, Bainbridge, Candy, Woody, Hardy, Faustine, Dinnie, Hannah, Ira, Jan, Keegan, Zsa-Zsa, and herself. No one had gotten lost.

Still cradling Keegan, Abbie stepped onto the ferry dock. She pointed across the bay. "Look, Keegan," she said. Far, far away was Fire Island, a hazy gray streak at the horizon.